The Holiday Club

ASHLEY MANLEY

Copyright © 2025 by Ashley Manley.
All rights reserved.
No part of this publication may be reproduced, distributed, or transmitted in any form or by any means, including photocopying, recording, or other electronic or mechanical methods, without the prior written permission of the publisher, except as permitted by U.S. copyright law.
This is a work of fiction. Names, characters, places, and incidents either are the product of the author's imagination or are use fictitiously and any resemblance to actual persons (living or deceased), places, buildings, and products is entirely coincidental.

Identifiers:
ISBN: 979-8-9996111-0-9 (paperback)
979-8-9996111-1-6 (eBook)

Book Cover by Elise Stamm, Blue Heron Graphic Design | Interior graphics from iStock

First edition: October 2025 | Ashley Manley

Editors:
Victoria Straw (developmental)
Kaitlin Slowik (copy edit)
Sadie Tabolt (proofread)

To Vale, who never turns down watching a cheesy Christmas movie with me.

A Note From Ashley

Last year, my daughter and I watched Christmas movies every day for an entire month. Somewhere between scenes of artificial snow and Christmas miracles, I wondered if I had a Christmas story in me. Then a thought: Why not try? Now, here we are.

As I sit around my pink Christmas tree watching my favorite movies again this year, I hope you enjoy the story of Hollis, Jay, and Marv as they experience the holiday season in the most unorthodox of ways. Please note there are a few instances of explicit language and scenes of romance (parts of Thanksgiving/Ch. 10 and December 7th/Ch. 12).

Merry Christmas! XO, Ashley

October 30th
Hollis

"Repeat after me." Kat's tone is as sharp as the lines of her angled bob and pressed black pantsuit as she pauses outside of the familiar conference room, her manicured fingers on the handle of the door. "I, Hollis Hartwell, will not walk out of this room again without being a free woman."

I roll my eyes—this is the fourth litigation meeting where she's tried this psychological pep talk. Yet here I am, still legally married to my bastard of a not-quite ex-husband after a year of these ridiculous meetings.

Not a free woman.

"Does this kind of bullshit mantra recitation ever work?" I ask, tugging at the collar of my pumpkin-covered sweater, perfectly on theme with the season and all the glorious festivities that await me if I survive the next hour. My stomach churns when I catch a glimpse of Ryan through the window of the door to the conference room, smugly relaxed as he talks to his attorney.

"It would if you repeat it," Kat snips, not waiting for me to respond before jerking the door open and giving the room a cool, "Gentlemen."

Reluctantly, I follow her; Ryan has the nerve to smile as I take the seat across from him.

It's hard to believe once upon a time I thought that smile was charming, but it must be; we wouldn't be in this room if it wasn't.

I would venture a guess that married men without charming smiles can't usually convince the nurses they work with to abandon their scrubs and bend over a vacant hospital bed otherwise. Easy on the eyes, says all the right things, and enough ambition to make any woman feel like they've been chosen. It's this lethal combination which makes Doctor Ryan Hartwell who he is: an asshole wrapped up as something pretty. It's not like I can blame them for falling for him. Twenty years ago, I did too.

"Let's get to it, shall we?" Ryan's attorney slides a paper across a table that probably costs as much as Kat does for two billable hours. It only takes a glance at the words *yearly holiday rotation schedule* before deciding I want to light everyone on fire and watch them burn.

"Is this a joke?" I ask through gritted teeth, glaring from the ridiculous document in front of me back to Ryan's arrogant face. "You want to rotate holidays by the year?"

Kat puts her hand on my arm—like I don't know I'm supposed to be playing it cool like she's coached me. Like I didn't hire her with all her sharp lines, bold shades of lipstick, and expensive pantsuits to take care of this. Like she believes I'm really going to *walk out of here a free woman* if this is the game he's playing. I yank my arm away from her, blood boiling. To hell with playing it cool. To hell with him.

I didn't want an ugly divorce. Despite my husband's multiple affairs, I didn't even know if I wanted a divorce—I thought we could work through it. Thought I could forgive and forget, and he would be the same Ryan I married. But as much as I tried to force us back together for a year, there was no coming back from what he did.

The first five years of our marriage played out like a honeymoon on repeat. Ryan built his career as a doctor, I had a column for a local newspaper, and we used every vacation day we earned in the quietest nooks and crannies we could find. Together.

Then came the kids, and as much as I loved being a wife, I loved motherhood more. I embraced it all. The sleepless nights, the potty training, the hard transitions. It was as if being a mom was who I was always meant to be. I left my job at the newspaper to focus solely on the four perfect children we created and started a blog called *Home with Hollis* to document every recipe, holiday tradition, and scary step of the motherhood journey. Women loved it—I loved it—so much so, a few years ago it led to a full-time opportunity at a magazine writing about those very same things.

Everything was perfect. I wrote us perfect. But now I know, perfection was the lie of the screen and keyboard.

Behind the scenes, I now see Ryan was drifting. His hours got longer and later, but I always chalked it up to doctor life. Being so busy with the kids, I never cared or worried. But the day I showed up at the hospital to surprise him with lunch and found his pants around his ankles and a nurse on her knees eating a little lunch of her own, there wasn't enough bleach in the world to erase that image from my memories. After that, the truth came out about the others—nearly a dozen. A train wreck with cars that just kept piling up one on top of the other. There was no coming back from it.

After a year of trying to put us back together, we separated. Now here we are, paying an exorbitant amount of money for a year of litigation that has gotten us absolutely nowhere. Two years since we shattered, and it still seems impossible to escape the shards of him.

Ryan interlaces his hands behind his head, cradling it as he leans back easily in his chair. It squeaks with the movement. I wish it would collapse, reassemble as an evil robot, and impale him.

He says nothing.

"Ms. Hartwell," his round-faced attorney says in his stead, four strands of his combover slicked to his forehead. Years of marriage only to have it end without Ryan even being the one to say the words. *Pussy.* "My client feels that with your terms of getting the house, more than he wanted to give of his retirement and savings—"

"He's made more money than me," I snap, clenching my fists on the table. "I only went back to work full-time four years ago, *Ryan*. Half of the retirement *we* saved isn't outrageous."

"Hollis," Kat hisses.

"After I spent years taking care of our kids *and* him so he could build his career," I argue. "Or did you forget that part, Ryan?" I cut my eyes to him. "Too busy screwing your way around the hospital to remember the wife at home washing the shit stains out of your underwear?"

"Hollis," Kat snaps, more firm.

"No." I keep my eyes glued to him. "Fuck you, Ryan. We've been rotating the holidays since we separated a year ago and you've never complained. What the hell do you want them for anyway? You're always working." With a flick of my wrist, I slide the ridiculous custody schedule across the too-big table toward them. "Over my dead body."

I grind my teeth; Ryan looks smugly bored.

Asshole.

"Because of your financial terms," his attorney continues,

adjusting the wire-rimmed glasses on his nose before shuffling through papers, "Mr. Hartwell has adjusted his schedule and feels this arrangement of holidays—all spent with one parent for the entirety of the year—will allow more easily for plans to be executed. Traditions, vacations, etcetera."

I give Kat a wide-eyed look; I'm a lion trapped in a cage. I know myself well enough to know if I speak again, I'll never stop.

"My client," Kat says, much more calmly than I could have pulled off, "has requested a fair split of assets. After being a housewife for years and focusing on their four children, none of her financial requests were outlandish. As Mr. Hartwell knows, Ms. Hartwell has always enjoyed the holidays. A yearly rotation would cause emotional turmoil for all involved. Ms. Hartwell, yes, but also their four children."

She continues to talk—to plead our case for not wanting a yearly holiday rotation schedule—but I'm down a mental spiral. Who does this? Ryan doesn't care about holidays. I'm not sure he's ever planned a single event for any of them. Christmas trees annoy him. Parades are too crowded. He can't even pronounce poinsettia correctly, for God's sake. I've always done it all. Loved it all.

"It's unnecessary," Kat says with finality. "If we set a normal rotating schedule of holidays now, there will be plenty of time to plan whatever vacations and traditions your client has in mind."

Ryan leans toward his attorney and whispers behind a cupped hand.

"If your client is unwilling to accept these terms," his attorney says, clearing his throat, "Mr. Hartwell wants to sell the house."

My spine goes ramrod straight as my jaw drops.

Sell the house? The room starts to spin. The kids love the house. I love the house.

Kat looks at me. I must shake my head because Ryan's attorney slides the proposed schedule back across the table.

Ryan smirks. He's got me, and he knows it.

"All holidays for a year," his attorney fills in as I once again read the paper—every holiday, festival, and date listed out with Ryan's name in bold next to them. "Should the holiday fall on a Monday, the long weekend before is included. Same with Friday holidays. And, as we live in Springer, North Carolina, the town dubbed Christmas Village USA, this will include all festival days in the town's peak Christmas season—which kicks off tomorrow with Halloween and ends with New Year's Eve. It includes every weekend for November and December as well as the entire week leading up to Christmas."

Dread takes a physical form in my throat. My favorite time of year. My favorite traditions. We live in a magical land where Christmas doesn't come for a day, it comes for two full months. A national newspaper dubbed Springer with the title Christmas Village USA just over a decade ago due to the prevalence of lights, cheer, and over-the-top schedule of traditions that make our town more magical than the North Pole. We don't just celebrate Christmas in December; festivities kick off with Halloween and last for two solid months.

And he's taking them.

The whole damn season.

I read the final lines. *The proposed schedule will go into effect immediately, with Mr. Hartwell getting the remaining holidays and festivities for the rest of the current calendar year.*

The blood rushes from my face. I'm going to vomit.

"You want this year?" I can barely breathe. Barely get the words out of my mouth. "Starting with Halloween? That's tomorrow, Ryan."

"That's correct." His attorney clears his throat. "Per the terms, Mr. Hartwell will pick the kids up from school today and have them through the entirety of the weekend and every weekend for the remainder of the year, as noted, to celebrate the holidays with his children."

I reread said dates, none of them fully registering.

The pumpkin sweater against my skin suddenly feels like it's burning my flesh off. Tomorrow is Halloween. *Tomorrow.* The kids and I all have animal costumes. I was going to be a cat. Jack a bear. Millie a pig. Ava a kangaroo. Owen a snake. They would trick-or-treat around our neighborhood; I would pass out candy—the full-sized bars our house has been hailed for—and then we would all go to the town's kickoff Christmas event to greet Santa, watch the costume contest, and light the town tree.

But this means none of that.

My eyes go to Ryan, desperate for him to show mercy. His face stays savagely stoic.

Not having the kids for the holidays—for the traditions that have become part of who we are for the last ten years—might as well be a dagger straight through my chest. But if I say no, mediation will continue, as will the drain on my bank account due to Kat's insane hourly rate. I make enough money at the magazine to pay the bills, but I couldn't afford to buy the house on my own. If I don't do this, I could lose it, along with my mind.

I look at Kat.

"You should take it," she says, in a low, yet firm, voice.

"But—"

"No 'buts,' Hollis. He's going to keep dragging this out. I know how you are with the holidays, but figure something out. Celebrate on different days with your kids. Take the extra alone time and do something for you. It's not worth it."

Celebrate on different days? Do something for you?

Every word feels like it's drowning me. That defeats the whole purpose and strangles every ounce of magic out of the season. Not to mention my job, especially this time of year, is focused on writing about kids and family. How the hell do I do that without kids or a family?

I open my mouth, but Kat talks over me.

"Leave this room a free woman, Hollis."

I don't have a choice. I feel it in my bones and see it all over her face. I need to let this end. Let him have the win so we can all move on with our lives.

I grab a pen and hover it over the line, forcing myself to sign. Life drains out of me with every looped letter of my name.

Ryan and his attorney shake hands. Make small talk. Laugh. We all stand—like a marriage of fifteen years didn't just end and life as I know it get obliterated with my name on the dotted line—and shuffle toward the door. I want to cry but hold it in. I'll wait until I'm in the parking lot and the safety of my minivan to have a proper come apart.

Yet I can't stay quiet. I can't let it go.

I grab Ryan's arm—the arm I thought would hold me up until one of us died.

"Why are you doing this?" My eyes search his face for a glimmer of someone I used to know. "You don't even care about the holidays."

He looks at me and pulls his arm away, tugging at the crisp cuffs of his white dress shirt.

"But you do," he says easily, the brown eyes I once thought were so warm now replaced with ice. "You went after the money, Hollis." He shrugs, adjusting the knot of his tie. "You hit me where I hurt, I hit you where you hurt."

Not only has time revealed Ryan as a piece of shit husband, it has also shown that he cares much more about money than I ever imagined possible. When I open my mouth to explain how wrong he has it, he strolls away, clapping his attorney on the back as they make their victory march down the hall.

Kat starts talking, but I can't hear a word of it because the tears don't wait for the minivan; they fall early. Not for the man I once loved—those shed and dried long ago—but for a season he's stealing out of spite. The memories I won't get. The joy. The traditions.

And once the tears start, they don't stop.

Not on the drive home or through the entire bottle of wine I drink that night before I go to bed.

Not the next day when I put on my black bodysuit cat costume and full face of makeup.

Not as I sit on the front porch with our bucket of full-sized candy bars, which I eat most of as I scare costumed kids off with my chocolate-mouthed sobs.

Not as I try to figure out how I'll ever survive this season without the four people I love most in this world, nor how I'll ever deliver my annual series of articles dubbed *Holidays with Hollis* when not one piece of me knows how to celebrate without them.

Halloween
Jay

The woman crying in the bowling alley wouldn't be so problematic if she wasn't doing it so loudly and from a seated position that has her encroaching into our lane. Dressed as a cat.

If I pretend she isn't there and bowl my turn, I'm an asshole. If I ask her to move, I'm also an asshole. More than caring if I come across as an asshole is the fact that interacting with a strange woman having a public meltdown is the last thing I want to do. The last thing I'd bet any man wants to do.

"My money's on a government diversion," Marv says with raised eyebrows from behind the rim of his plastic cup of beer. His round face framed by hair sticking out like he's been electrocuted makes his statement either more or less absurd.

"From what?" I ask, as my ball pops up the return and I slip my fingers into the holes, eyes glued on the weeper. Her cries have been replaced by a blank stare down the lane, shifting her presence from sad to spooky.

"From what?" he repeats with an incredulous scoff, eyes pinging around in their typical maniacal fashion. "Everything,

Jay. How many times do I have to tell you they are into ev-er-y-thing?" He presses his lips into a tight line to drive his point home. "Why do you think they have these fancy new computers to keep score in here?" He flicks a finger against the screen of the dated computer monitor, but I don't argue.

A monotone voice comes over the speaker: "Okay, Bowlers, it's officially seven o'clock on Halloween, meaning the tree has been lit in the town square and Santa has arrived in Springer. Christmas has officially arrived in Christmas Village USA."

When the previous Halloween music is replaced by "Jingle Bells," per town tradition, the woman lets out a loud sob.

I grimace and glance around the bowling alley. The only other person besides Marv, the cat, and myself is the acne-faced, teenage boy who works here, obliviously useless as he scrolls on his phone. An annoying sense of obligation claws at me. Like it's my duty as someone not crying to ask this basket case what's wrong.

I just want to bowl—like we do every Halloween—and have fun—like we do every Halloween—without all this.

"She's not bleeding," I say, unmoving as she drops fully onto her back. Her head rests in her own lane as her long black spandex-covered legs stretch into ours. Bowling ball cupped in my hands, I glance at her assigned table: one beer, barely touched. She's not drunk. "She's probably fine."

"Could be menstrual," Marv says between sips. "The females hide the blood making it nearly impossible for the males to detect. Trust me—" He gives me a knowing look. "I learned the hard way."

I don't ask him to elaborate.

The woman pulls herself to a seated position, wipes her nose with the fabric of her catsuit, and glances toward us, catching us staring. *Shit.*

I force a smile, and gesture at her with my ball.

"Oh," she says, standing with another sniff. Her eyes are bloodshot, her nose is red, her painted-on black whiskers are smeared across her cheeks. "Sorry, I-I don't usually do all this."

"All good," I say with a tight smile, stepping up to the line and preparing to bowl.

If I curve it to the right it should—

"It's just," she continues, taking a step toward our area and using a tail I hadn't noticed to wipe her eyes. Judging by the way she's moving into our space, she's a talker. I mask the audible groan building by clearing my throat.

"Sorry, you want to bowl." She blinks at the ball in my hands. "My kids love bowling." Her eyes fill with water. "My divorce finalized yesterday."

I cut my eyes to Marv; he's frowning. She doesn't notice.

"And my ex-husband wants yearly holiday rotations. *Yearly*." When she laughs, it sounds like an actual cat being held underwater.

Our silence seems to encourage her, because not only does she keep going, but her voice gets louder with every word.

"What am I supposed to do with that?" she demands. "Who does that? I love Christmas. I love all holidays. We live in Christmas Village USA, for God's sake. He did it on purpose. After *he* fucked a nurse." She blows out a frustrated breath, and the cat ears on her head droop to the side. "Lots of nurses, actually." Now she's yelling. "And I gave birthday blowjobs!"

She's furious, dressed like a cat, and it takes every ounce of willpower for me not to laugh at her shouted *blowjobs*.

"And my job." She groans—loudly. "I'm a writer. I write about motherhood. And holidays. And every year I write about family Christmas traditions. I can't do it. I just can't. I'm a cat without the rest of my litter." She lets out another cry as she twists her tail in her hands. "Santa just marched into Springer with his Christmas tree-carved jack-o'-lantern and lit the town

Christmas tree and had the town costume contest, and I'm here alone. I can't write about this." She makes a disgusted face. "I'd rather die."

I've seen the Santa jack-o'-lantern and ridiculous contest—which Santa always wins—and the tree lighting. They're nothing to die over, but I don't dare tell this crazed feline woman that.

"I mean it," she continues. "Just kill me now with your bowling ball. Smash it over my head and shove a pin through my heart. I won't feel it. Just—"

Whatever she's saying next comes out too wet and garbled for me to understand, but she's stepped to the side enough I can bowl my turn.

So I do.

Right down the middle for a strike.

I celebrate with a coordinated spin and clap. "Rock's on fire today, Marv."

He grunts. "You practice all year? Against the rules, you know."

I chuckle, adjusting the antler- and bell-adorned hat on my head before swiping my beer from the table and eyeing the score screen—fourth strike in a row.

"College intramurals," I remind him with a grin, taking a sip of the subpar lager. It lacks flavor, has zero depth, and I'm pretty sure they need to clean their lines. Bad beer is better than no beer, so I take another sip.

"Bullshit," Marv says, standing. He adjusts the tuck of his Holiday Club bowling shirt at the elastic waistband of his sweatpants before investigating his ball with his flashlight. "That was twenty years ago."

He's right—I bowl like hell every September and October just so I can kick his ass come Halloween and—

"What are you looking for?" the woman who refuses to

leave asks Marv as he shines a light in every crevice of his ball. She's now standing at the end of our U-shaped seating area, curious look on her tear-streaked face.

"You with them?" Marv's eyes narrow; despite the harsh tone he uses, she makes no effort to leave. He sighs. "Fine. Gunpowder. Evidence. Anything they can use against me in a court of law."

Pleased he doesn't detect anything, he pockets the light in his sweatpants and takes his ball, sending it down the lane to slam into the pins. Bastard gets a strike.

The cat stares. Sniffs again.

She wants to talk.

No thanks.

"Well, I guess I'll leave you to your game," she says with a weak smile and without moving. Against the backdrop of the over-the-top, tacky, holiday-themed bowling décor and the now-cheery Christmas music blaring through the speakers, she resembles a human-sized stray cat on its last life.

"Okay," I say, with a lift of my beer. "Cheers."

She inches back into her space as Marv and I each take another turn.

Out of the corner of my eye, I see her take a sip of her beer before picking up a ball and lobbing it down the lane; it goes so slowly I wonder if it might stop. Instead, it drops with a sad *thunk* into the gutter, barely mustering the gumption to roll the rest of the way.

Her shoulders slump, along with the fuzzy black tail attached to her costume, and "Frosty the Snowman" plays over the speakers. When she starts crying—again—the cat ears give up their fight of staying on her head and fall to the floor.

Marv looks at me like I'm supposed to do something about this.

"You," I snap in a whisper.

He holds up his palms, eyes wide like *no way in hell, dude.*

I consider what to do, pressing my index finger and thumb to the center of my mustache then sliding them away from each other. Twice.

I take one reluctant step toward her. Then another.

Next to her, I clear my throat, ignoring every warning bell telling me this is the worst idea. I don't want this kind of drama. I don't want *any* drama. It's the whole reason I'm here with Marv.

And yet, despite all that, I can't let a woman in a catsuit one day post-divorce cry to the tune of too-early Christmas carols.

"You know," I say, shoving my hands into the pockets of my jeans as we watch her pins reset down the lane. "It's ridiculous in a world where 'Thriller' exists, 'Frosty' is playing on Halloween."

She blinks her watery gaze to me. To my antler-covered hat. My mustache—*thank you for noticing.* At my red-and-white striped bowling shirt, her eyes linger on the embroidery spelling out The Holiday Club.

"It's rude, really," she says with an almost smile. "Don't they know it makes unassuming women everywhere turn into blubbering idiots?"

I rock on my heels. "Happens all the time."

She laughs fully, wiping her eyes with her hands—her once whiskers now unrecognizable—then looks at my shirt again. "I'm sorry for interrupting your game. You a team?"

"A club," I say with a grin. She looks at me with big wet blue eyes; I take a step back. To be nice: "You want to join us?"

"Whoa," Marv barks, pouncing to a stand. "We do not know this woman, Jay."

I pin him with a look. It's one day, one game; we can both handle that.

I think.

"Fine," he grumbles at me. To her: "You wearing a wire?"

Here we go.

"Uh." Her brows pinch as she sniffs again. "No . . . ?"

"Don't mind him," I tell her, rubbing a hand along my jaw. "Marv spends too much time on the dark web."

Marv grunts and she nods slowly, taking him in.

I know what she's thinking because it's the same thing I thought when I met him just over five years ago. He was sitting at the bar drinking a pilsner, complaining how the holidays are a time the government takes advantage of large gatherings to steal information. Between his radical ideals, patchy beard, and shirt tucked into sweatpants paired with sandals and socks, I thought he was nuts.

I still do.

But less than a week later when the normal Halloween festivities of trick-or-treating followed by a Santa welcoming and tree lighting for the town dubbed Christmas Village USA took place—where I would no doubt be annoyed by the crowd and tired of questions about my marital status, life choices, and overall living situation—Marv and I went bowling and The Holiday Club was born.

"You're a-a club?" She looks from Marv to me. "A bowling club?"

"A holiday club," I correct, taking my ball from the return rack. I step up to the line, adding over my shoulder, "We get together every weekend from Halloween to Christmas."

I send the ball down the lane for an eight-two split and mutter a swear.

"Do you bowl every time?" she asks.

"Halt," Marv commands with a hand in the air. "No more questions until we know she's safe." He rummages through his bag and pulls out a security wand.

The woman's eyes go wide as Marv approaches her, waves the wand around the entirety of her body without asking, and listens intently for a spike of *beeps*.

When he doesn't detect a wire or explosives, he gives me an approving nod—like I'm the one who thought this woman was trying to bring down a sleepy bowling alley in the middle of the Blue Ridge Mountains—and returns the wand to his bag.

"First and last name?" he barks.

"Uh. H-H-Hollis," she stammers, so wide-eyed I cough to hide my laugh. "Hartwell."

Marv produces a tablet from his bag, typing her name aggressively into whatever database he uses for his endeavors.

"Jay Randall," I introduce myself, shaking her hand as she gapes at Marv. "And to answer your question, we bowl on Halloween," I explain. "The rest of the holidays, we do different things."

She sits in one of the chairs, tail draped over one thigh, and looks between Marv and me, taking a plastic cup of beer I offer to her.

"Different things?" she asks, thoughtful look on her face before taking a sip. "You're anti-Christmas?"

I grab the ball from the return with a chuckle.

"Anti-tradition expectation." I bowl and knock only one of the two pins down, muttering another swear. "I love Christmas." I flick a dangling jingle bell on my hat as proof. "But it stopped feeling fun." I shrug. "We started The Holiday Club."

Her spine straightens, look on her face telling me she doesn't approve. "You don't think traditions are fun?"

"Not the ones other people expect."

She frowns.

"Don't you miss your family?"

"I see my family plenty the rest of the year," I say wholeheartedly and with a half smile. "These days are just for us."

Her eyes go to my hand, no doubt in search of a ring she won't find.

"You aren't married?"

"Nope."

"Why?"

That . . . is a loaded question.

"Never got around to it."

Her eyes narrow. "Never got around to it?"

I take a sip of my beer. "Seems that way."

She makes a disbelieving sound. "You have to *get* around to it."

It's hard not to laugh.

"According to the fact I'm not married, I'd say I don't."

Her eyes bounce all over me.

She doesn't ask about Marv's family. She either assumes he doesn't have one or is too scared of who they are if he does. It's the right move; she's not ready for all that.

"There's no point of Christmas if you don't have traditions."

"I have traditions," I say with a raise of my beer.

She scoffs. "Beer and bowling is *not* a tradition."

"It is if you say it is."

Marv raises his head from his tablet, piping in with, "Traditions were invented by the government as a form of mind control for large subgroups of the population—found her. Hollis Hartwell." She frowns. "Age thirty-nine. Born on February seventeenth. Writer for *We Women* magazine. Four kids, delivered vaginally." He glances at her with raised eyebrows. "Impressive. Legally separated for one year—divorce finalized yesterday as mentioned—from one Ryan Hartwell who is a medical doctor and graduate from Duke University. Hollis has one speeding ticket from the early 2000s and two overdue library books." He puts the tablet back in his bag and says with a satisfied tone, "Clean."

"Wha—how did you?" Her wide eyes bounce from Marv's bag to me then back to Marv.

"I know more than them," he states like it's common knowledge, nonchalantly taking a sip of his beer.

"Anyway," she continues, eyes lingering on Marv a second longer. "Trick-or-treating before the Christmas tree lighting ceremony happening right now four miles away is a tradition. Annual costume contests. Getting married in a white dress in the same church your parents did. Taking vows. Those are traditions. This—" She sniffs. "Is fun. There's a difference."

"Ah. So you're saying traditions aren't fun?" I counter, taking another sip of my beer to hide my smile.

"Of course they are," she says, testy.

"Really?" I raise my eyebrows. "That tradition of matrimony seems to be a real hoot."

She glares at me. A few strands of hair fall across her stained face. *Cute.*

"So you just take the holidays and do whatever you want?" she asks, judgmental edge to her voice. "Do you work? Or is holding down a job too traditional for you?"

"I'm a dabbler," I admit with a grin and lift of my cup. "With a passion for beer."

Her eyes narrow again. "Like a bartender?"

She doesn't mask her *grow the fuck up* expression.

"Beertender," I correct.

"Okay," she drawls, flicking her skeptical gaze to Marv. "I'm guessing he won't tell me what he does?"

Marv looks at her like she's just pulled a pistol out of her pants.

I chuckle, lifting a bowling shoe–covered foot to a vacant chair and propping a forearm across my thigh. "I'm not sure I even know. What about you? You said you were here for work?"

She nods, tucking a strand of loose hair behind her ears. Now that she's not hysterical, even with the face paint, I can see she's pretty. The light brown hair spilling from the top of her head like a fountain frames a heart-shaped face, full lips, and big blue eyes. The costume clinging to her slim body doesn't leave much to the imagination, which I very much like.

"I'm a writer," she says as Marv steps up to the line for his next turn. "For a women's magazine, as your friend so disturbingly shared. I write articles for the online division. Tips for vacationing with families, routines to make life easier, summer activity guides, stuff like that. Every Christmas I write about family traditions. Now without my kids . . ." Her voice trails off as fresh tears fill her eyes. The pins explode from Marv's bowl before he steps next to me. I pull my foot from the chair and stand upright. "I don't know if I can do it. I love Christmas. *Traditional* Christmas. The baking of perfect cookies for the bake sale and the parades. Without my kids, I don't want to celebrate any of it." Her voice cracks and she sniffs.

Beer fills my mouth and I still, holding it in my cheeks until she continues.

"That's why I'm here. Trick-or-treating was a disaster." She looks down at her costume and her lips start to quiver. "I thought skipping the Santa costume contest and tree lighting to come here would spark an idea on something else to write about. My attorney told me to have fun. I came to the bowling alley." She starts to cry again. From somewhere in the bowling alley, actual jingle bells ring, prompting her to groan-wail, "But Christmas is everywhere." She drops her head with a loud sob. "My ex-husband got my kids for Christmas along with my will to live, so now I just-just-just—" She finishes the sentence with a cry and whole-body shake, causing beer to slosh over the rim of her cup and onto her catsuit.

I slip the drink out of her hand, set it on the table, and give Marv a *now what?* look.

He clears his throat. "I need to check the vents."

The man plotting to take down the government flees from the crying woman. *Wimp.*

"You know," I say, sounding a bit like a hostage negotiator. "Holidays are just made-up dates. You could do whatever you usually do with your kids on different days."

She uses her entire hand to swipe the tears off her cheeks. "I can't ask the town to relight the tree to a day more conducive to my ex-husband's assholish plans." She shakes her head. "No. Without my kids, there's nothing. What's the point of doing it alone? Of-of even getting a Christmas tree?" Her eyes are wide and wild. "I'm skipping it. All of Christmas. You're right."

I have never once suggested skipping Christmas.

She reaches for her beer and takes a long sip, a look on her face like she's formulating a plan.

"I don't understand why anyone would want a holiday without all the regular traditions," she continues. "That's the whole point. The whole entire point of Christmas is the tried-and-true traditions. It's doing the things you'll look back on to remind you of how loved and special you are because they happened the very same way at the very same time with the very same people every single year. It's like morning coffee. It doesn't work if it happens at three in the afternoon, you know?"

I consider answering but she doesn't even give me enough time to open my mouth.

"I can skip it all this year. I will. Maybe you're onto something. And Kat." *Kat?* "I could—I don't know—tag along with you two for the season. I could write about it. A Year Without Christmas. Something like that." She bites her lip, eyes bouncing with her thoughts. "Too negative."

"You know Christmas still happens without parades, right?"

She scoffs. "But is it the same? Is it—that's it. I've always talked about the importance of traditions as I experience them, this year I could show what happens without them, in turn proving their necessity to the season. Show everyone how dire it makes things." She looks at me, face filled with hopeful desperation. "You could show me what you two do, and I'll prove it's not real Christmas. Not really. Please."

I swallow a hefty gulp of beer.

"Can't you tell the magazine you want to write about something different?"

"I've done it every year for four years," she says, offended. "I don't half-ass my commitments like my ex-husband. Plus, I love my job—especially this time of year. I've built a community. Moms everywhere depend on me. And" —she looks at me with what I would dare call judgment—"I'm not some kind of-of-of—" Her eyes bounce all over me again. "Easy on the eyes, mustached Santa dabbler like you. I'm a professional. I can do this. I will."

My eyebrows lift. "Easy on the eyes, eh?"

"That's not the point." She huffs out a frustrated breath. "The point is that I need your help."

Marv returns from his vent quest, hands on his hips, brows hitched high on his head.

"Marv doesn't like new members," I tell her.

"Eh. No wire," he says, looking from her to me. "What do I care? Jay? You good with it?"

Fuck no, I'm not good with it. She'll change things. Write

about them. Marv and I have a great thing going—these last five years have been the easiest holiday seasons of my forty years of holidaying. I invited her to bowl one game, not be part of the club.

She's already had multiple meltdowns. Already attacked me for not being married. Already put words in my mouth I most definitely did not say.

"Please, Jay," she begs with a bounce and her hands pressed together. "You'll barely notice me."

Judging by the crying and all the talking, I find this highly unlikely.

"We do things outdoors," I tell her. "Even when it's cold."

"I have a coat."

"We stay out late. End up in weird places."

"I'll drive myself."

"No kids allowed."

"Are you deaf?" She huffs. "I don't have my kids. That's the whole, stupid point."

Dammit.

"Sometimes we pick up women." This is a lie—Marv scares all women off. "That a problem?"

Her eyes bounce all over me—again. Pink splashes across her cheeks. "I can be a wingwoman."

She's not backing down. I either have to be an ass and point-blank tell her no—which might lead her to crying again —or just go with it. Just let her in. Risk the ruin of this good, easy thing we've built.

No.

Absolutely not.

I look at Marv; he shrugs.

I grab the ball for my next turn and look at her. I hate how sad she looks. Hate that I even care.

"Fine."

I pull my arm back, and she squeals as I swing it forward. The ball slips from my hand and slams into the gutter without hitting a single pin as I mutter a swear.

"Marv, Jay, I'm Hollis Hartwell. Officially." She's beaming as she thrusts her hand out to Marv. "Newest member of The Holiday Club."

Marv looks at her hand with a disgusted frown. "No touching."

Her eyes widen and hand drops. "Right. Sorry."

"You like hot peppers?" Marv asks, digging into his pocket. She presses her lips into a tight line as he pulls out a little plastic bag of peppers. "Over 100,000 on the Scoville scale."

Her chin pulls back slightly as she eyes the bag. "I'm good."

Marv harrumphs, plucks one out, and drops it into his beer then pockets the rest before taking his next turn.

"Marv's into conspiracy theories," I explain as she watches him.

"The hot peppers?" she asks with raised eyebrows.

I laugh over the rim of my beer. "Into those too."

She studies him intensely. "I see."

Marv gets two strikes in the tenth frame to win the game, pumping both fists into the air with a gloating, "Cheating can't save the sheep."

I laugh, resetting the computer for the next game and add Hollis's name. Whether or not she'll show up at the next club meeting, I have no clue, but she's here, clearly going through something, and it's Christmas. Even with my unorthodox approach to the season, I have a heart.

I'll let her bowl. Let her have this day and this win that she seems to need for the next forty-five minutes.

Hollis, to her credit, doesn't cry anymore. She also doesn't shut up. She tells us about each of her four kids—repeatedly—

and shows us more photos of them on her phone than I've seen of my six nieces and nephews combined. I know the oldest, Owen, plays soccer, the youngest, Jack, is in kindergarten and likes dinosaurs, and the middle two are girls, Ava and Millie, and like painting fingernails and Lisa Frank—whoever that is—which thrills Hollis because she loved Lisa Frank when she was their age. Her ex-husband is a doctor named Ryan and couldn't keep his dick in his pants.

She's animated, the worst bowler I've ever met, and charming as hell. Her ridiculous stance on traditions unnerves me, yet when she pauses from talking, I'm anxious to hear what she'll say next.

When we're done, we stand under the lights of the parking lot. Marv next to his spray-painted box truck, Hollis in her catsuit next to her minivan, and me next to my SUV.

"How do we know what to do at the next meetup?" she asks, pulling her keys out of her purse.

I slide my phone out of my pocket. "You give me your number, and I'll send you a text."

Without batting an eye, she takes my phone out of my hands and enters her information, cute smile on her face when she hands it back to me, pausing slightly. Our eyes meet for a split second, the slightest hint of pink splashing across her cheeks before she looks away.

"Thank you for letting me tag along," she says politely. "And I'm sorry about the cat costume and all the crying."

Marv and I just nod, watching as she hurries into her minivan, tail swishing behind her as she goes. I'm not much of a phone guy, but if I were, I'd call her, right now as she's driving away, just to hear what she'd have to say. If she wasn't just crying and carrying on about her ex-husband, I'd probably ask her to go out to dinner with me.

Tonight.

"Think she'll show?" Marv asks as she disappears down the road.

I look at him with a wry smile. "Crazy ones always do, Marv."

The Season of Struggle?
By: Hollis Hartwell

When I was a child, my mom filled our Christmas mugs to the brim with cocoa, our stockings with toys, and our hearts with cheer.

Every December first, my dad hung the same strands of lights along the roof and put the same glowing Rudolph in the front yard. My parents lugged their same aluminum folding chairs with frayed webbing to the same spot along Main Street to watch the Christmas parade. The same vintage ornaments went on the tree as we watched the same movie about Santa Claus. Every Christmas Eve, we walked around our town's small festival of lights only to come home and unwrap matching pajamas.

They are some of my favorite memories from my childhood. I grew up with Christmas being synonymous with love. Now, as a mother, I have had the honor—and duty—of cultivating those very same tradition-filled memories with my own kids.

But this year, the season has arrived to find me a bit wounded. A bit lonely and Grinchy, if I'm being honest. Being a mom who thrives on a chaos-filled schedule of the town's festivities while wearing bold Christmas garb with my kids by my side and proving my love by doing the things we've always done, I have nothing. Namely, my kids, who will be spending every single tradition and special day without me.

As I sit at my computer writing this, it occurs to me I might not be the only woman struggling this season. Not the only person questioning the meaning of the season and the traditions we've crafted. How do we keep smiling when the key players don't show up? Can the Christmas show go on if life changes the way it is inevitably designed to do? Will those around us know we love them even if it's not our face they see on Christmas morning?

After a lifetime of every holiday season being as predictably beautiful and magical as the last, this year, whether I like it or not, is different. Because of this—because I can't bear to do the things I've always done without eight additional hands reaching for me, I've decided to do none. I'm skipping every tradition to see what, if anything, is left. What magic remains if we divorce ourselves from the things we've always done to celebrate?

While my Christmas-loving town gathered like the Whos of Whoville for the annual tree lighting and Santa costume contest, I, like the Grinch in his cave, opted to go in a different direction: to the local bowling alley. It took the entire first half of my time there to think about anything other than all I was missing.

Then the unexpected happened: Two strangers with a unique brand of holiday cheer befriended me and invited me to join a game. I'll admit, I don't yet understand how they smiled so easily knowing all they were missing out on just miles down the road, but they did. Without reservation or regret.

I have doubts about the longevity and authenticity of this kind of Christmas spirit. Joy born from randomness and the desire to not conform instead of from a passion for preservation can't work, can it?

And if it can, what does that mean for someone like me who has spent their life clinging to the traditions of parades and dates on a calendar?

Take heart, wary mamas, for better or worse, we're in this season together.

November 7th
Hollis

Jay
Tomorrow at 5. Dress warm. I'll send the address.

Marv
mnojk

Hollis
I'm guessing that's Marv.

Jay
He has an untraceable flip phone and types in code to throw the bots off.

Hollis
I would expect nothing less.

Marv
pqrsdede wxymnotu tghdepqrde

Hollis
Wow.

When Jay texted last night, I wasn't sure if I'd be able to do this. On the drive to the address, I listed every single reason to turn around. Aloud. Twice. Most involving Marv, who is either a danger to society or harmlessly insane.

But curiosity and loneliness make a potent cocktail when mixed, because, despite my best efforts, here I am. And, as nervous as I am—as ridiculous as this all feels—something about Jay made me want to show up.

If I hadn't been a complete soppy mess in a cat costume when we met, I would have sworn there was an undertow of interest in the way he spoke to me. The way, despite how completely unhinged I must have looked in that bowling alley, when I was speaking, it was as if I was the only person there. Like he was hanging on to my every word. Ryan never listened to me like that, magnifying Jay's behavior even more. Unsettled me even more.

Still, a week with my number, all I got were the instructions in a group text with Marv, leading me to believe I was very much reading into things.

Eyeing a vacant barn—a perfect place to hide a body—I pull the key from the ignition, my knee bouncing maniacally against the steering wheel of my minivan as I chew my lip. *What the hell am I doing here?*

Jay appears, same absurd antlered hat on his head he was wearing at the bowling alley, and my chest tightens.

This is real.

I'm meeting strange men at a strange place in the name of skipping Christmas.

Jay pulls a large door open on the barn, steps inside before emerging with two horses hitched to a wagon. He looks like one of Santa's helpers about to head west in a live game of *Oregon Trail*.

Whatever this is, I can't do it.

I shove my key back in the ignition, turn it, then remember: home will be worse. It will be empty because my kids are with Ryan. At the Christmas parade I've been going to for over a decade. Without me. It hollows me out.

"You can do this, Hollis," I mutter, yanking the key back *out* of the ignition and using every ounce of energy to get my body out of the van and moving toward Jay.

"Hello," I say when I'm next to him, sounding a bit terrified as I eye the horses and him. Because I am. Because only clinically insane people do this.

"Hello," he mimics with a slight smirk, leaning against the wagon and crossing his arms over his flannel-clad chest, amused spark in his green eyes. "Wasn't sure if you'd show."

"Me neither." A laugh puffs out of me, but I don't shy away from his gaze. "I hope it's okay."

His eyes bounce from the beanie on my head to the laced-up boots on my feet. "Wouldn't have texted you if it wasn't."

"Oh." What is *that* supposed to mean? "Okay."

He adjusts the straps on the horses then does a walk-around inspection of the wagon, whistling the tune of "Rudolph the Red-Nosed Reindeer" as he does.

He's got this rugged *I don't give a damn* vibe. Over his top lip, the most absurd mustache I've ever seen in real life and an exact match with the dark hair peeking out from the bottom of his hat. At the bowling alley, he appeared to be fit, but the thick layers of tonight reveal nothing about his body.

And yet.

Against every traditional standard of which I have ever judged appearances—even with the mustache—he's attractive.

Despite the stupid hat, maybe even hot.

I eye the two very big horses and the connected wagon covered in red chipped paint. "I didn't expect horses." He makes an acknowledging sound mid-whistled tune but offers no information. "Is it safe?"

He puts a thermos and stuffed bag on the bench of the wagon.

"We aren't going far," he says with a smirk.

He does that—smirks—constantly. I noticed it last week. It's like he's in on every joke the world has ever told. There I was having a stage-five freakout about my life in a bowling alley, and he just stood there, amused. Like the cardboard cutout of Santa holding a bowling ball wasn't shredding my cat-costumed heart into smithereens.

I glance around, letting it sink in I'm here as I try to figure out how I'm going to spin this for my weekly article.

The Holiday Club was good in theory, but it's not who I am. I write about motherhood, and there's not a child in sight. Plus, if I'm not celebrating the season with our traditions, I'd rather hide in bed. Crying. When I sat down at the computer after bowling, I decided I'd tweak my content from last year and reuse it for the magazine, but after years of writing my truth to women readers, I felt like a fraud. Fake. I decided to write my truth and my fingers obliged, openly confessing to the keyboard that I was going into this season broken.

The week that followed wasn't as bleak as I expected. When I picked the kids up Monday afternoon, it was like a switch flipped and the situation became significantly less dire. Though there weren't the usual holiday songs or decorations surrounding us, I stopped crying. I took them to school and made dinner every night. We played board games and did homework. I *almost* forgot about Christmas.

"*How was the tree lighting? And the costume contest?*" I had asked over Sloppy Joes.

"*They plugged the lights in like they always do,*" said Ava in her seven-year-old toothless voice.

"*Was the star on top?*" I asked.

They all nodded, bored.

"*What about the costume contest?*" I pressed. "*Who won?*"

"*The mayor dressed as Santa,*" Owen said flatly. "*Like every year.*"

"*Isn't that funny?*" I laughed. "*He wins every year.*"

Owen shrugged, talking around a mouthful of food. "*Seems pointless to have a contest, doesn't it?*"

I looked at him. Blinked.

"*It's not pointless,*" I argued. "*It's tradition.*"

They all started talking about something else.

But today? Today I knew I was dropping the kids off this morning only for them to get picked up by Ryan who would take them to the Christmas parade. I cried in the car line until the school resource officer tapped on my window to make sure I was okay to drive.

I told him everything; he told me I was stopping the flow of traffic.

Here's the thing people don't tell you about getting divorced: It's humiliating. Humiliating to tell people you couldn't hack it as a wife. Humiliating to tell people your husband stepped out on you because you clearly couldn't keep him satisfied. Humiliating to know that the man you thought you'd love forever based the custody schedule on what would hurt you the most.

Aside from the humiliation, it just fucking sucks.

When I found myself pouring a glass of wine with lunch to drown out the pain of missing the first Christmas parade with my kids in my decade of motherhood, I knew I'd show up tonight. I had to. If for no other reason than to fill the Christmas tree–sized hole in my heart.

A slamming door turns my head.

Marv strolls toward us from his creepy box truck, his eyes pinging around the sky in earnest. He's wearing sweatpants, a puffy coat, and sandals over socks.

On his head: a set of large headphones.

In his hands: a walkie-talkie and antenna.

He is a complete weirdo.

"Hello, Hollis," he says with a too-loud voice as he approaches. "Brought my ham radio." He climbs directly into the back of the wagon, raising his eyebrows as he gestures at me with his equipment. "Speak without censorship."

I look back at Jay; his mustache twitches.

Knowing he wants to smile makes me fight one.

Where Ryan is a doctor and looks like one—sharp, clean, expensive—Jay is his polar opposite with a mustache and coat lined in frayed edges. Ryan is a polished fancy suit, Jay is a pair of blue jeans, worn to perfection.

I eye the antler-adorned hat on his head; Jay is as far from my ex-husband as it gets.

"Hollis?" Jay asks, smirk on his face as I blink. Twice. "I asked if you're warm enough."

"Right," I say, cheeks scorching; I was staring. I pat my jacket as if to remind myself I'm wearing it. It's late and the sun is setting. Even though it's bone-deep cold, my nerves are buzzing; I doubt I'll notice. "I'm fine."

He helps me into the wagon where he and I sit on the bench at the front. With a slight slap of the reins, the horses lurch down the trail. The wheels moan as we move, and the muffled clip-clop of the hooves and Marv's random mutters form a mismatched symphony. For the first few minutes, neither Jay nor I say anything.

"You have a wagon," I finally say, breaking the silence. "And horses."

He looks at me, reins loose in his hands. "I have a *friend* with a wagon and horses. He runs rides out here every year. Lets me and Marv take it out before it all kicks off in mid-November."

I eye his hat. "Does every Holiday Club meeting involve you wearing that hat?"

"No." The trail curves from a grassy field into a wall of trees as the horses clod us into the shadows, and his mouth curves into a smirk. "But the ladies love it."

"I doubt that," I say dryly.

"Oh really?" He swipes his tongue over his bottom lip. "Why's that?"

"I think you have commitment issues," I tell him, matter-of-fact. "And I have no idea what kind of woman would be attracted to that." Translation: I felt a certain attraction to him at the bowling alley, which made absolutely no sense and therefore led me to spending the week talking myself off of that misdirected ledge of wondering if he felt any of what I felt during my public display of lunacy. "I thought about it a lot this week," I continue. "You don't like traditions. You aren't married. You dabble in beer, whatever that means." I pause to let him explain, but he says nothing, same ridiculous lift of his lips as I continue. "Those things combined with your above-average looks lead me to one conclusion: You can't commit. Life gets boring—it's the nature of the beast—including relationships and traditions. And people like me endure it—try to salvage what's left and keep things together—while people like you move on to something new and novel. Nontraditional. Therefore, the women you go after must be—" Even his blinks are amused. "Confused."

He lets my observations hang between us, looking at the horses before back at me. "You thought about me a lot this week, huh?"

I guffaw. "The fact that's what you took away from all of what I just said proves my point."

The wagon bumps over a rock in the road, making me fall into him before jerking myself upright.

"Well, Hollis the Writer," he says in a low, smooth voice, leaning toward me so his shoulder purposefully touches mine. "Maybe you're right." I let out an audible *See!* as he continues. "But you should know, if I have commitment issues, maybe it's because the right person hasn't come along. Maybe there's nothing wrong with spending holidays not doing what everyone else does—without reservation or regret." His eyebrows raise. "And maybe my relationship status and holiday beliefs have nothing to do with one another. Maybe you don't know a damn thing about the kind of woman I'm attracted to." When I think he's finished, he adds, "At all."

I open my mouth, snap it closed, then scrub my tongue across the back of my teeth.

"Fine," I say, ducking from a low-hanging branch as we jostle through a pothole.

He smirks. "Fine."

Behind us, Marv shouts into his ham radio, "Earth to space. Earth. To. Space."

"He always do this?" I ask Jay, as Marv sweeps the antenna through the air.

"Last five years," Jay says, smiling but serious.

Five years of the two of them doing this. I can't figure it out. It seems lonely, but they're both oddly content. When we were bowling, they laughed the whole time. Easily. Out here, laughter has been replaced with a serene lull. Like they're immune to pressure and stress. Oblivious to anything happening outside of this wagon. To the fact a parade is happening filled with noise and cheer.

I look back to Jay and he looks right back, almost challenging.

His whole position on holidays unnerves me. Like because they bowl and come out here to play cowboys, my float watching makes me ridiculous.

"You have a family?" I don't know why I sound like we're in a fight.

"I do," he says, attention on the horses. "An older sister, Caroline, and a younger brother, Brent. Both married with kids. And my parents." He flashes another white-toothed grin. "Also married with kids."

I snort a laugh despite myself. "What are they doing tonight?"

"They went to the parade. Depending on schedules, sometimes they get together for dinner. You know how it is with kids—a little chaotic to plan all that sometimes."

The wagon jostles through another pothole.

"And you're fine with that?" I ask. "Them doing everything without you?"

There's nothing but the sound of horse hooves, wagon creaks, and Marv's random shouts for nearly a minute.

Finally, he asks, "What was it like after everything fell apart with your husband? With other people, I mean?"

I don't bother to hide my shock at the question but can't seem to find a word to adequately answer. Because it was awful. Because I wanted to crawl in a hole and sleep for seventy-four years. Because every gathering was like a rehashing of the worst thing that had ever happened to me. *He cheated on you? How did you find out? You poor thing! How can we help? What do the kids think?* Over and over and over. It was easier not to be around anyone than constantly retell the story.

I half-truth with: "Fine."

"Hm." His side-eye makes me think he smells my bullshit.

"Well, with my family—who is wonderful, extremely well-intentioned, and very opinionated—there are always comments, which lead to drawn-out conversations about choices I've made and how they think I can make better ones." He switches the reins between hands. "The holidays seem to magnify them." He shrugs. "There's no bad blood—they want me to be happy. Sometimes they forget that doesn't only look one way."

While his response shines a little light on the situation, it unleashes a dozen more questions than answers. I want to ask, but something tells me not to. Like if he tells me he won't want to, and I'll be no different than everyone else he's avoiding.

"I don't get you," I say, putting my hands under my thighs for warmth.

"You don't know me," he responds. "And there's a blanket in the bag. We're almost there."

I start to argue but bite my tongue, pulling the blanket out and spreading it across my lap before focusing on the horizon. We're in those last minutes of the day where everything looks a bit blue. A bit sleepy. The trees are bare, the moon is full.

"KD9JDF, do you read me?" Marv shouts from the back of the wagon. "I repeat, KD9JDF, do you read me?"

I look over my shoulder. One of Marv's arms is overhead with the antenna, the other is holding the radio to his mouth.

My kids would love him; it catapults me to them. Wondering if they're at the parade. If they're having fun. If they miss me. If they even notice I'm not there.

"You're quiet," Jay says. "What's in that chatty head?"

I tuck my chin to my shoulder, waiting for the emotions to pass. For the burn in my eyes and lump in my throat to dissolve.

"My kids," I finally admit. "How strange this all feels. How untraditional."

He chuckles. "Which part?"

From the back, Marv shouts, "Are you on Mars?"

I snort a laugh. "All of it."

Jay shifts the reins between hands, studying me a split second before looking back at the horses.

I pick at a thread on the crocheted blanket.

"Tell me who you are," he says. "And not your kids and ex-husband. Something else."

He looks sincere; it's startling.

"Okay." I hesitate. "Well. I like the color green. And pancake houses. Not diners but places that specialize in pancakes. There's about a million of them in Gatlinburg. And combined businesses that make no sense. Know what I mean?"

He looks at me, mustache pulling up on one side. "Like, over in Ledger there's that birding store and boxing gym. And the mechanic and notary. A peddling paradox."

He chuckles.

"Okay, what else?" I tap a finger against my lips. "I haven't dated since my separation over a year ago. My husband and I weren't dating at the end. Or liking. Or touching. Or—" Jay looks at me, expectantly. "That was . . . not good." I rub a hand across my forehead, trying to swallow the bitter taste filling my mouth that comes with knowingly sharing a bed with a man who has screwed other women. "Sorry, you don't care about that. I really like when I recognize characters in movies from other roles. I'm kind of an expert at that. I can just spot them—like, *hey! I know that guy from that weird scene in that one movie!*" I grin. "Your turn."

He blinks several times.

"A difficult act to follow but prepare to have your mind blown. My favorite color is dark blue," he says with mock seriousness. "I think it's impressive more squirrels don't get hit by cars. Someone needs to improve the durability of the hard-shelled taco. I appreciate a hazy IPA. My favorite time of day is sunrise." He pauses, glances at me, then adds, "And I like the shape of your face."

"The shape of my face?" My eyes narrow. "What does that mean?"

"It means what it means."

"Who says that?" I huff, pressing the back of my hand to my apparently pleasantly shaped cheeks. *Why am I warm?* "That's a ridiculous thing to say. I've never heard that before in my life."

"It's shaped like a heart." He's so calm it makes me more flustered. "And I like it." He shrugs. "And just because you've never heard it doesn't mean it's ridiculous."

I balk at him while opening and snapping my mouth closed.

Is he flirting with me?

Then: *Do I want him to be flirting with me?*

Judging by the echo of flutters in my belly at the comment and my body's sharply fluctuating temperature in his presence, I'd say I do. That I'd like that.

Oh, God.

I *want* Jay to flirt with me. At once, I feel completely exposed. I tighten the blanket around me like some kind of armor and force my focus toward the horizon line.

Rolling hills slope toward the sky before dripping down. I don't know if it's the cedar trees or the chill in the air, but it smells like the holidays. Despite the fresh pep in the pounding of my pulse, it's comforting. Grounding.

Marv asks the radio if he's speaking to the mother ship.

"Close your eyes," Jay says.

"What?" I respond, incredulous. "No."

Everything about his presence has my whole body on high alert. Like a schoolgirl with a playground crush.

Close my eyes? What could he possibly need me to close my eyes for? And Marv's back there in the wagon, he coul—

"Holiday Club rules," Jay says. "When we turn this corner up here"—he gestures with his chin—"we'll be there. Close your eyes."

I look at him.

Swallow.

Feel my chest tighten.

And do as he says.

The first few seconds drag on, every beat of my heart harder than the last, but then I relax. I rock with the movements of the wagon as the chill of the air claws at my skin.

He gives a low *whoa* that stops the horses before taking my hand—briefly—and guiding me out of the wagon.

Standing behind me, mouth close to my ear, he says, "Open."

I do.

And bring my hands to my mouth with a stunned laugh.

Around us, glowing like conic stars grounded on Earth are at least fifty trees—maybe more—dripping with strands of white lights. Hundreds of tiny bulbs surround each one. On the ground, paper lanterns glow.

"What is this?" I ask, consumed by awe as I take several slow steps.

In the newness of night, the lights are so bright our faces are fully lit.

"Old Christmas tree farm," Jay explains, grabbing a thermos and three mugs. "Family thing. The parents died and kids didn't want to run it. Tree business didn't make much money, but they loved the trees—and Christmas—so they started doing this a few years ago, taking donations for local charities. Do the lights because they love them." He pours what smells like hot chocolate into the mugs. "Marv," he hollers over his shoulder. "Drink."

Jay hands me a mug as Marv walks up, pulls his headphones off, and looks at the trees.

"This many lights confuses the extraterrestrials," Marv says, matter-of-fact, as he drops a tiny red pepper into his drink before taking a slurpy sip. "Probably why they do it."

He looks at me, Jay, then wanders into the trees.

"Tell me," I say, blowing the steam from my cup as Jay and I fall into step together, sauntering through the trees. "What is Marv's origin story?"

Jay chuckles. "Way he tells it, about ten years ago, he was married and working in some kind of computer tech job when he got abducted by aliens. Nobody believed him. His wife left. He became Marv."

I pull my chin back. "You don't care?"

"Care?" he asks with a laugh. "Aliens didn't take me." His smile stays as he drinks from his mug, some of it clinging to his mustache. It's inexplicably cute. "He's a good guy," he continues. "Fun to bowl with. Keeps me entertained. Doesn't care that I'm a forty-year-old unmarried beertender the way some people do," he teases. "No pressure."

Every word he says is genuine, refreshing, and completely captivating.

I take my first sip of my drink and it burns my throat; I gag. "This is not hot chocolate."

"Adult hot chocolate," he amends with a press of his lips. "I add whiskey."

I snort a laugh and take another sip, the burn less shocking the second time going down.

We stop in the middle of the trees, light surrounding us in every direction. It's like a fairy tale. A Christmas fairy tale. Beautiful, and much to my surprise, better than any float in any parade. A place where a man might drop down on one knee and propose to the woman of his dreams or a couple just starting out might fall a little bit in love.

"Thank you for letting me force my way into being here," I say, looking from the trees to him, a million little lights reflecting in his eyes. "My kids would love this."

"You should bring them," he offers. "When they're with you. Or next year."

Bring them?

Every other year of the holiday season has every square of the calendar filled with things we do every year on every day. This is the opposite of all that. This is quiet. Simple.

"I have the International Space Station," Marv announces from deeper in the trees. "KD9JDF. Do. You. Read. Me? I'm in the lights, ISS. Follow the light."

Jay and I stand there, looking at each other for one, two, three heartbeats. And though it's been a while, I don't know him at all, and I'm extremely out of practice, I like looking at him. Like him looking at me.

I tell myself it's just the trees. Just the effect of the lights and my loneliness playing tricks on my head and my heart. Whatever it is, for the first time in years, standing in this once-was Christmas tree farm in the middle of the hills, I'd love nothing more than the man standing next to me to take my hand in his and tell me he's happy I'm here.

"These trees suit you, Hollis the Writer," Jay says, taking a step toward me, close enough I notice.

My breath stills. Our eyes hook and hold. *What is happening?* He reaches a hand toward my face—slowly. I cannot breathe. Just over my skin, he pauses.

Then pulls a twig out of the yarn of my hat and my breath gushes out of me when he shows it to me.

"From the wagon ride," he says.

"Ha." My blood moves through my veins a little faster.

"Twigs."

A small smile curves his mouth, and we stand in a brief silence. Him cool as the breeze with lights reflecting brightly in his eyes, me with a foreign feeling making my skin feel too tight.

"We should go make sure Marv doesn't get abducted again," he says around the rim of his mug, amused lilt to his voice.

I nod, press my cold palms tightly against the warm mug, nerves settling.

"That would be quite the Christmas story," I joke, following his lead.

We stroll through the trees until we find Marv, then the three of us walk together, sipping our adult hot chocolates until they're empty.

On the wagon ride back to the barn, the conversation is light. No more family or traditions, just three people in the woods. Marv tells us about a guy he bought a ham radio from who had pigeons living in his house and newspapers covering the floor. Jay laughs easy at everything he says, giving me a wink right before he asks him to tell me another story. Like he's saying a secret *get ready*.

Nothing about tonight with these two strangers is ordinary or makes sense, yet the sadness I've carried with me seems to melt—just slightly—like an icicle in the morning sun.

I don't remember to miss the parade I didn't go to again until I get home and open my computer.

The Promise of the Parade
By: Hollis Hartwell

The wonderful thing about parades is they don't always happen. They're special. They require planning and anticipation. Demand us to make decisions on the perfect chair to bring and perfect spot along Main Street to put it.

Then, when the stars align, the music will start, the floats will roll out, and everyone from the town plumber waving a jingle bell–covered plunger to the dentist dressed as a giant molar with elf ears will roll by your seat and spread Christmas cheer.

But what if the parade eludes us? What if it's too early, too late, or the wrong day altogether? What if, like me, your heart is too dinged and dented to attend?

As kind and merry as the parade is, it will not reschedule. Its promise is to carry on. It won't care if it's your chair along Main Street or someone else's. It is the lesson of tradition: be here or not, the show must go on.

On the day when eager faces lined the annual route and waited for Santa to cruise by, I found myself next to my unexpected holiday guides being dragged to the middle of nowhere. Only it wasn't nowhere at all; it was a Christmas tree farm turned modern marvel, which effectively stole my breath and stopped my heart. And, because I want to be nothing less than honest with you, I wasn't even really dragged. I just went.

Sure, my fuel was an abominable mixture of sadness and loneliness, but there was also curiosity too. A lingering *what if?* dancing at the blurred edges of my thoughts and propelling me toward strangers and an unknown destination in the woods.

There were no crowds. No fire engines blaring their sirens. No kids catching candy. It was not showy. The magic there was of a different variety. Like the pull to shake a snow globe then being unable to look away until the last flurries settle on the bottom, this unassuming display demanded attention and stillness.

Tucked in the trees, it did not care when I showed up. I didn't need the perfect seat nor spot to put said seat because, much to my surprise, every angle offered views. Its only requirement was darkness and was only enhanced by silence.

But it wasn't the unpredicted beauty of the location that had me lying in bed staring at the ceiling long after I returned home; it was the realization of how much I enjoyed it. How much I wish someone would have been there to hold my hand and look at me the way I looked at the trees.

Despite my current aloneness, I wasn't lonely there. Instead, an incipient flame of hope lit within me. Hope that maybe—just maybe—there's a chance I'll make it through this season after all.

But with that hope came a dark cloud of doubt at how lasting my wonder will be. Was I only amazed because my sadness needed something beautiful, or will I look at the floats from my familiar spot along Main Street next year and dream of standing between glowing trees?

It's hard for me to imagine a season that ends in me feeling fulfilled without a parade, but even more so, to imagine never seeing these trees again.

I read once it's the forsaken who have the biggest room for growth. If true, this season without everything I love may prove the perfect time for a spurt.

November 14th
Hollis

Jay
Tomorrow at 6:30. We'll be inside. We can ride together?

Marv
ghijkljkl dpqrghituvde defmnopqr pqrsadefdetwxy

Jay
Suit yourself. Hollis? Want me to pick you up?

Hollis
Depends. Will there be a wagon?

Jay
Guess you'll have to send me your address and wait and see.

Hollis
I like surprises.

Jay
I like surprising.

> **Hollis**
> Explains the hat.

Jay
I think you like the hat.

> **Hollis**
> I think you want me to like the hat.

Marv
apqrde wxymnotu twmno pqrsdewxtghimng

> **Hollis**
> Can you translate that, Jay?

Jay
I can but won't. Marv, I'm telling the government where you live.

> **Hollis**
> Yikes.
> But also, what did he say?
> Jay?

~

"I think that's the mom—No, the *grandma* from *Parenthood*," I observe around a mouthful of popcorn from the passenger seat of Jay's SUV. "That one." I point at the large face through the windshield. "Bruce Willis's wife. Or ex-wife?"

Bruce Willis's face appears on the drive-in movie screen as Marv's silhouette cuts across it, arm swinging a metal detector over the ground in front of him.

"Never heard of it," Jay says without looking at me from the driver's seat.

"Never heard of it?" I scoff. "We're watching *Die Hard* for Christmas—which is not a Christmas movie, by the way—and you've never heard of *Parenthood*?"

He looks at me, smirks, and says, "Nope."

As if scripted, a Christmas tree appears and festive music plays through the speakers of the car.

He gives me a look like, *told ya,* and I shoot one back: *go straight to hell.*

Only three other cars—including Marv's box truck—are parked in the grassy field of the drive-in theater I didn't know existed.

Possibly because it's in someone's backyard and we had to pass a dozen hand-painted ENTER AND GET SHOT signs to get here. Mostly because the rest of the town is gathered in the park to watch a movie—a real Christmas movie. My kids included.

Without me.

"Everyone else is watching *It's a Wonderful Life* in the park —together—and you're here. I don't get it. Why not just go where everyone else is?"

He tosses a piece of popcorn in his mouth and glances from the screen to me. "I don't like that movie."

I gasp. "You *what*?"

He shrugs. "George Bailey kind of sucks."

Another gasp. "He *what*?"

"Sucks." He doesn't look away from the screen. "He complains. Helps people then whines about it. Just a pain in the ass, really. And he has that voice." His nose scrunches in disgust. "Kind of nasally, you know?"

I open my mouth, close it.

Open my mouth, close it.

Open my mouth, give up.

Because, maybe, he's not wrong.

We watch Bruce Willis work to save the day for a few minutes. A topless woman is dragged across the screen.

Christmas movie, my ass.

I shove another handful of popcorn in my mouth.

"Plus," Jay continues, "it's warm in here. I hate sitting on those blankets, they always get damp. And the volume is never loud enough. It's kind of bullshit."

I suck in a sharp breath. "Bullshit?"

He glances at me, hand of popcorn stilling before he tosses it in his mouth. "Kind of, yeah."

"That's a sacrilege," I accuse, only half meaning it. It might actually be bullshit. I've been doing it for so long because it's what we've always done, I've never even considered my opinion. It's tradition. Repetition required, no matter how unpleasant.

I do not admit my kids have said the same thing minus the explicit language for the last two years. Nor do I tell him they weren't even excited when I asked them about the parade this week.

"*How was the parade?*" I had asked them over dinner.

They all shrugged.

"*There was hardly any candy,*" Millie complained in her sing-song voice. "*And it's always the same floats.*"

I shot her an incredulous look. "*Of course it's the same floats,*" I explained, annoyed that the nine-year-old already noticed. "*That's the whole point.*"

She shrugged; Owen started talking about a kid who got in trouble for talking back to his teacher; the parade ceased to exist.

My eyes are back on the screen. "You didn't tell me Professor Snape is the villain." Jay doesn't respond. "From

Harry Potter," I clarify. He shakes his head; I blow out a disbelieving breath. "Half-Blood Prince? Professor of the Dark Arts?" Blink. Blink. "Bad guy but ultimately not really because Dumbledore trusts him and he loved Harry's mom?"

He gives me a blank look. "Never heard of him."

I groan, spot another familiar face on the screen, then perk up. "Stop it. Snape's right-hand man is Trivette from *Walker, Texas Ranger?*"

Jay's silence is revealing.

"I know what you're thinking," I admit with a sigh. "You're thinking, Hollis is annoying to watch a movie with. I already know, thankyouverymuch. I really am trying to do better. My ex-husband told me I ruined movies because—okay, wait. Bruce Willis is going to bring down all these guys—" I pause to let Bruce Willis shoot a construction zone filled with thugs. "In an undershirt and without wearing shoes?"

When I look at Jay, he's smiling.

I frown around a mouth of popcorn.

"Why are you looking at me like that?"

"You're very charming."

Three things happen at once with his statement: my face heats, my heart skips a beat, and I want his hands all over me. That last one clearly a sign of how neglected of another's touch my body has been.

"I . . ." *have never once been called that in my entire life.* It's too pathetic to admit. Instead: "Okay."

He turns his attention back to the fight happening on screen, and the light plays across his features as he tosses his antler hat onto the dash and rakes a hand through his thick head of dark hair. At the top it's wavy and tousled.

This observation starts a chain reaction; I can't stop looking at him. I absorb every little detail like a kid looking through a toy store window planning a wish list for Santa.

One perfectly angled jaw.

Two green eyes complemented by a dark blue long-sleeved fleece, rolled up his forearms, which somehow flex from the simple movement of him grabbing handfuls of popcorn.

Six lines splaying from his eyes when he smiles.

Even the mustache—that stupid thing—is intriguing.

He's annoyingly attractive.

I wonder if this is who he always is. If he looks like this every other day of the week. What his hands would feel like if they—

"For someone who told me they gave their asshole of an ex-husband birthday blowjobs the first night we met and never stops talking," he says, raising two good eyebrows as he looks at me. "A lot goes on in that head of yours you don't say."

The darkness is a blessed thing for hiding the blaze on my flesh that is burning me alive. The first night I met Jay I was a wreck and could have easily read into his kindness and attention just as much as I could have read into the way I swore he looked at me last weekend while I was under the influence of romantic Christmas trees and spiked hot chocolate. Divorce and dating at this age make my feet feel slippery and my judgment untrustworthy. I have no way of knowing if my reaction to him is driven by my desperation for companionship this season, a silly me-sided crush, or if he's feeling whatever this is that I'm feeling.

Plus, I'm not just one person, I'm five, including my kids. I can't just chase after the first man who reminds me I have a neglected vagina. I have to make sure it's right. For all of us.

Instead of saying any of that, I deflect.

"Why do you have the mustache?"

He chuckles. "Because I like it." He sweeps popcorn crumbs off his hands and strokes said mustache, playful expression consuming his face. "The ladies *really* seem to like it." I ignore the new kind of wondering that unleashes in me. "And that's not what you want to ask."

"It was," I argue.

He looks at me, smug and reading my lie. "Then why are you asking?"

"Fine." I chew my lip, debating how to redirect this conversation to something closer to what I want to know. "Do you date?"

He sends me a sideways look and a smirk. "You asking me out?"

I scoff. "No."

"Do *you* date?" he tosses back.

I bring a hand to my throat. Tug at the neck of my sweater. Fumble with the dial of the AC. *Why am I hot?* "I'm a mom."

"Ah," he says, turning his attention back to the screen; Bruce Willis found another gun. "Moms don't date, I forgot."

"That's not—that's—" I huff a flustered breath, bothered. He's a nice man being nice to a lonely woman by letting me be here. That's all this is, and I'm not ruining it by acting on a weird, illogical crush. "I'm thinking of going online. To date. Men. Romantically."

I have never once considered that.

"Really?" He looks at me, curiosity consuming his face. "Online?"

I pull my shoulders back with a sniff. "Maybe. It's what I've read people do at my age. I don't know how to meet men."

Even my skeleton is mortified by this ridiculous confession.

His brows pinch as he fills his mouth with popcorn. A piece misses and lands on his lap; he makes no effort to clear it.

"And I was thinking since we are spending time together —" I clear my throat. "You could give me pointers."

"Really?" Jay says around a mouthful of popcorn. "About what?"

I swallow. "What men like."

He stares at me; eleven years pass. "I see."

"You don't *see*," I defend. "There's nothing to see. You asked if I date, I told you I might and—"

"Online strangers."

I let out a sharp exhale. "Most people are strangers when they start to date, where they meet is irrelevant."

He reaches into the back seat for the thermos and refills our adult hot chocolates. "Your profile say *must love annoying traditions?*"

I blow out a flustered breath as he tops off my mug. "I'm ignoring you."

He chuckles, relaxing into his seat before taking a sip of his hot chocolate. He drapes his free arm over the center console that separates us.

I stare at it. Because I'm some kind of psycho, I put my hot chocolate in a cupholder and put my arm next to his, close but not touching, his stupid flexing forearm radiating a heat that's almost magnetic. I'm already warm in the close quarters of the vehicle, so why I'm craving this closeness to him is beyond me.

On screen, a dead body appears with a message written on it in red. Professor Snape's character is not pleased.

I scoot my arm a fraction of an inch toward Jay's. When they touch, I stop breathing. *What am I doing?*

"Hollis?" he says.

I clear my throat, eyes glued to our single line of contact. "Yes?"

"You're staring at our arms."

"Oh." An embarrassed heat consumes every square inch of me. "Am I? I was admiring this center console." Being the idiot I am, I knock it like a door. "This is a nice design. Solid. Sturdy. Room for snacks. And trash bags. And baby wipes." His lips press into a tight line. "Not that you have a baby." My eyes ping around his virtually spotless SUV, a far cry from the crumb-covered minivan I drive. "Or trash."

"It is a good center console," he says, not bothering to hide his smile.

Dear Bruce Willis, please shoot me with your gun.

"You have an appeal," I blurt, awkward. "Even though you're opposed to marriage, I'm surprised you don't have someone serious in your life. That's why I was asking. About the mustache. And the dating."

"I never said I was opposed to marriage," Jay says, not looking at me as bullets blast across the screen. "I said I never got around to it. I had someone once. Years ago. Someone I thought I could see myself with long-term. Maybe marry."

"What happened?" I ask.

"She couldn't get over my career choices." He finally looks at me. "And she married someone else."

He's not smug. Not amused. The look on his face is serious, vulnerable, and a little bit telling.

All I can find: "Oh."

Marv taps on the window prompting Jay to roll it down. *Yippee-ki-yay, motherfucker*, blasts through the speakers before a loud boom rattles the whole vehicle.

"Found two dollars and forty-three cents, six bullets, and a wedding ring," Marv says, eyes bouncing between Jay and I. "Why are you two serious?"

Jay glances at me before saying, "Hollis is looking for internet boyfriends."

My jaw drops. Marv frowns.

"Don't do it," Marv says in an ominous tone. "That's how the sleeper Soviets are gaining traction." His eyebrows raise to his hairline. "They prey on the lonely and say all the right things before stealing your money and bugging your ballpoint pens."

Wait—*what?*

With that, he's gone, sweeping his metal detector across the ground as Jay rolls the window back up and looks at me.

"Why not date real men?" Jay asks, smug expression back in full effect.

"Real men?" I echo, annoyed. "Real men can be on the internet, first of all. But to shut you up, I'll clarify: I am open to dating if I meet someone whom I connect with and is okay with dating someone like me. Internet or otherwise."

Without breaking eye contact, he puts his drink in a cupholder and turns his head to fully face me, doing a villainesque stroke of his mustache with his thumb and index finger. I gift myself exactly three seconds of imagining what it would feel like dragging across my skin.

"Someone like you?"

My face heats. He does that. Takes one little piece out of a whole slew of things I say and clings to it like tinsel on a tree branch.

"I'm done talking about this," I snap.

"Tell me," he presses, leaning slightly into my space across the console. I back away but have nowhere to go. My head hits the passenger window. He's close; I'm sweating.

On screen, large lights are getting shot out. I recognize one of the police officers as the dad from the show with Steve Urkel from the '90s but keep the discovery to myself.

"Fine," I rasp. "I'm a mom. Who—" I clear my throat and look at my hands, any confidence shot straight to shit. "Who might not be very good at dating, as indicated by the fact my ex-husband sought out other women during our marriage. Who's a bit bruised by the holidays and still doesn't think *Die Hard* is a Christmas movie despite fully appreciating the five-star cast of side characters." I flick my eyes to him; his lips twitch. "I guess that's what I would say."

"Hm."

There's a long pause.

Jay raises a knuckle to my temple before dragging it gently down the side of my face, causing my breath to still.

"I would have thought you'd say something like—" He pauses, pursing his lips in playful consideration. "'Charming but married an asshole.' Or 'loves Christmas but has terrible taste in movies and traditions.'"

I want to laugh, but him touching me, complimenting me, lets only a slight hum come out of my mouth.

His knuckle slips from my face to my shoulder then whispers down my arm over the fabric of my sweater until it reaches my bare hand. He traces each finger. The spaces between them.

Then.

Interlaces his hand with mine.

It is embarrassingly innocent, but the connection of our palms is enough to cause a full body ache. I haven't been touched in such a purposefully tender way in a long time. I haven't held a hand besides a child's in years. Maybe that's what happened to Ryan and I: We stopped holding hands and our marriage went to hell.

"We're holding hands," I say, stating the obvious. Delighted as I am dumbfounded.

"We are." He squeezes my hand with his. "How do you feel about that?"

I clear my throat. "Um."

My *um* means one thing: I am so thirsty I would climb into the back seat with him and strip naked.

"I'm fine with it. It's good. Warm. You have warm hands. Big ones. Which means . . ." I squeeze my eyes shut, cringing at how badly this is going. "Big gloves."

He laughs softly, bending our elbows and angling his head

so he has a clear view of where our palms connect. "See how they fit?"

The curves of our two palms mold toward each other like a river to its bank.

He hooks his eyes onto mine. "I don't know if you're going to find that on the internet, Hollis. A fit like this."

Wait—*what?*

The rapid-fire *Tat! Tat! Tat! Tat!* of machine gun blasts through the speakers. Jay squeezes my hand before releasing it to retrieve his mug and sink back into his seat.

"This is the best part," he says, eyes on the screen.

While Bruce Willis saves Christmas, I cannot breathe.

My entire body heats like it's been blasted with a blowtorch, and my heart is pounding like it is actively trying to escape my body.

"What just happened?" I ask, higher pitch to my voice than usual. "Was that—was that something? The hand holding—were you—I don't know—" I can't bring myself to say flirting.

"You said you were going to date men on the internet, and I had the urge to know if our hands fit together before you do. They do. Now you'll know."

"I'll know?"

He shrugs, smirks, and barely pulls his attention from the movie as he says, "Looks like it."

At once, I'm annoyed. "Why do I need to know that?"

"Maybe you didn't."

I scoff. "So why do it? Why-why-why even—"

"I don't want you to date internet men," he says casually, flicking his eyes from the screen to me.

What?

His calmness amplifies my panic. I press the back of my hand to my face: hot.

Dammit.

"Why not?" I demand, at once pissed at him and how flustered he's making me. "What does what you want have to do with anything?"

I drink my hot chocolate in gulps for the whiskey alone. When my mug is empty, I drink it straight from the thermos, burning my tongue and making him chuckle. This SUV is too small. I roll the window down, blast of cool air barely helping.

He tosses more popcorn into his mouth. "I'm thinking of asking you out."

I suck in a sharp breath. "Asking me out?"

I can't breathe. I'm trapped. I peel off my sweater, revealing the tank top I'm wearing beneath it.

Once again, he looks at me, smirks, and says, "Thinking about it, yeah."

"*Thinking* about it?" I demand. "What is that supposed to mean?"

He brushes the crumbs off his hands and wads the popcorn bag into a ball. "It means I'm feeling things out and thinking about it." He flicks his gaze to mine. "A lot."

"You can't do that, you arrogant ass." I am fully outraged. "You can't just tell me that. Hold my hand and look at me and say all those things and have some kind of convoluted *thinking about it* mindset. What if I meet someone? What if I don't want to go out with you?"

He pins me with a knowing look as the credits start to roll and lets out a small sigh. "Well, if you meet someone, then I guess I have my answer, but for now"—he shrugs—"I'm waiting."

"Waiting?" I repeat. "What the hell for?"

"For you to be ready." He starts the ignition, using one hand to wave to Marv as he gets into his truck, metal detector in tow. "That was a good movie, right?"

He's completely nonchalant.

Like he didn't just say all that.

Like he hasn't made me dizzy with the thought of someone like him with someone like me.

"No, I hated it," I snap. "What does all that mean? What do I need to be ready for?"

He looks at me, amused tilt to his lips as he drives out of the lot. "Lots."

"Lots?" I echo, irritated.

I ignore whatever he says next, refusing to talk to him the whole drive home.

He wants to ask me out? Who tells someone that? Aren't you supposed to simply say the words with a firm date: Let's have dinner this Friday at 7 p.m.?

Whatever this sort of fuckery is he's playing, payback will be severe. I will crush him. I will pull a page from the book of Bruce Willis and physically destroy him, shoes or no shoes.

"Hollis," he calls as I'm walking up my front steps, still muttering swears under my breath. I turn and look. "For what it's worth, I love watching movies with you."

I stare at him; he drives away.

I wonder if he's smiling as big as I am.

Die Hard Is Not a Christmas Movie

By: Hollis Hartwell

I have spent a lot of time over this last week thinking about what makes a Christmas movie different than any other movie. Is it the setting of Christmas? Does Santa need to save the day? Is snow a requirement?

My personal favorite film of the season is about a loud family coming back together for the holidays where one of the grown children introduces a woman who doesn't quite fit with the rest of them. They aren't right for each other, disaster ensues, and yet, there is no villain. They are all good. Imperfectly human like the rest of us.

One particular scene spoke to me a bit more than usual this year. The family the new woman visits takes a photo in which she isn't included. I cried at that—I don't know if I ever have before. I sat on my sofa thinking *I know that feeling*. Know what it's like to want to fit somewhere and not. To be a bit clunky in my own skin.

I'm pretty sure I have spent the last two years of my life feeling this exact way. Wanting my marriage to work. Wanting everyone to be happy. Wanting my smile to look genuine when neither of the former were happening.

At the end of the day, our clunky girl finds someone who sees her—adores her—just as she is. It has nothing to do with Santa or even Christmas, simply a matter of her being at the right place at the right time with a man who is so different than her he's perfect. He doesn't play games. He just loves her. Even the parts other people don't like.

What if Christmas movies have nothing to do with Christmas and are simply just movies we need during the holidays? What if it's *Jurassic Park* on Christmas Eve or *Star Wars* on Christmas morning because those are the stories that challenge us to dream of things that seem impossible? What if movie night in the park under strings of lights was *Pirates of the Caribbean* and when we feel a bit lonely, we watch *When Harry Met Sally* while wearing pajamas of red and green?

Maybe the movie isn't about the movie at all. Maybe it's not even about Christmas. Maybe it's about more.

Die Hard is not a Christmas movie, but, perhaps in years when we need a distraction, it is. When the last thing we need is the reminder none of our traditions are what they used to be, it's the absurdity of a machine gun saving the day that pulls us out of our heads and into the moment like a well-chosen gift. Like a glimmering thread of cinematic magic.

Die Hard is not a Christmas movie, but it has the audacity to claim its spot in the season, demanding it be noticed by putting Bruce Willis's face next to Bing Crosby and Tim Allen as the tried-and-true symbols of yule. No matter how unlikely, no matter how much we may or may not agree with its categorization, here it is—with lasting power—leading me to wonder what else is out there making less sense but feeling like Christmas just the same.

Die Hard is not a Christmas movie. But maybe it is.

November 22nd
Jay

Jay
Busy night tomorrow night at Brew-Ha-Ha. Marv, can you get here early? Hollis, does 5 work for you? I'll send the address—it's on the outskirts.

Marv
wxydepqrs

Jay
Perfect.

Hollis?

You ignoring me because of what I said about George Bailey?

Marv
mawxyabde tghde ajklghidemnpqrs gmnot ghdepqr

Jay
Maybe. Or she's just playing hard to get.

Hollis
Sorry. I'll be there but I don't know what time. I had other plans come up. For after. That I'll be busy with. With other people.

Jay
Other plans? Holiday Club rules state there can be no other plans.

Hollis
Guess I'm a rule breaker.

Jay
Loves traditions yet breaks rules. Aren't you full of surprises.

Hollis
I told you I like surprises.

Jay
And I told you I like surprising.

Marv
pqrstghijkljkl ghdepqrde

∼

"Is this China meat?" Marv shouts from the kitchen.

"Local," I holler from my spot behind the bar. "From that farm near Asheville."

He grunts. The grill sizzles. The smell of cooked onions ensues and mixes with the scent of oranges and hops already in the air.

I pull out a sleeve of plastic cups, lining them along the bar for tonight's flights and flick my gaze to the door.

No Hollis. *Yet.* She'll show.

Despite how worked up she got at the movie, and the fact

she mentioned other plans in last night's text—which, I can be honest, irritated me—she'll be here.

I wasn't lying when I said I want to ask her out. I do. I've wanted to since she wedged her way into our bowling game. But she's a woman with a broken heart and a hang up on traditions. I have to wait, have to be sure she's ready, for her as much as me.

I hadn't planned on touching her, but she started talking about dating, and as much as I knew she was bluffing, I had to be sure. Had to confirm the spark I feel just by sitting next to her wasn't just my imagination.

It wasn't.

Thirty seconds of her hand in mine generated enough electricity to power every string of lights in Christmas Village USA.

I had to know; now I do. There's something.

And no matter what she says, the constant flush of her cheeks and adorable oversharing all say one thing: She feels it, she just needs more time.

Plus, I can read. And I do.

Everything she writes.

She's coming around.

The warmup twang of guitar floats from the band donning tropical poinsettia shirts on the small corner stage as headlights shine through the window.

A minivan.

I grin.

But when Hollis pushes through the doors of Brew-Ha-Ha Brewing, my smile falters. Because she's hot. Tight jeans, low sweater, new hair hot. And the way she's strutting toward me, she knows it.

"Hey," I say, setting the stack of cups on the bar.

Her usual light brown hair is in waves around her shoulders with new hints of blonde, and she's wearing makeup.

Light pink on her full lips and mascara framing her blue eyes. Little ankle boots and painted-on jeans make her legs look eight miles long. The neck of her red sweater is low, revealing a small line of cleavage I haven't had the privilege of seeing until this very moment. Every time we've gotten together, she's been cute—either dressed as a cat or casual—but this woman staring me down is downright sexy.

I rest my palms on the edge of the bar. "Wasn't sure you were coming."

When she's directly across from me, she sets her coat and purse on the bar and gives me a feisty look.

"I said I had plans *after*," she replies evasively.

My eyebrows pinch as she takes in the large room we're standing in. From the exposed wood of the ceiling to the windowed wall behind me showcasing the copper vats and pipes to the stone fireplace filled with stacked logs and roaring flames.

"This where you work?" she asks, her eyes going from the hat on my head to the vintage Rudolph T-shirt I'm wearing.

"It is," I tell her. "There's a private event tonight. Little different than usual."

She frowns and looks down at her outfit, confidence wavering. "Is it weird I'm here?" she asks. "A private event I'm not invited to?"

"Ah." I rub the back of my neck. "You're working with me."

"Oh?"

"It's a charity event for the animal shelter in the area," I fill in as she eyes the Doggy Donations box, high-top tables covered in papers and pencils, and the chalkboard sign that says Brews, Brats, and Barks. "Ticket gets beer and brats. We'll serve the beer, Marv's in the kitchen making the brats."

"Good evening, Hollis," Marv calls from the kitchen.

"Hey, Marv," she shouts, smile tugging at her lips. To me: "I've never been a beertender before."

"I know a guy." I tilt my head. "C'mon back and I'll show you how it's done."

She shuffles behind the bar, giddy pep in her step until she's beside me and I launch into beer mode. I show her the glasses and the taps, then give her the breakdown of the brews —all made in house—and let her taste each one.

I hold a glass to the tap, angling it slightly as I start to fill it. "This cuts back on the head," I explain, working to minimize the foam.

"Too much head is a bad thing?" she jokes. "Must have been what went wrong with all those birthdays with my ex-husband."

Instead of telling her I would gladly take that birthday gift, I laugh. She shrugs with a smile. So damn charming.

A tapping of claws and jingle of bells entering the room make us both look; my black lab trots into a space between the high-top tables and sprawls out across the floor.

"Goose," I explain.

"A beertender and dog lover," she says, almost playful. "You're full of surprises, Jay."

"Looks that way." I smile and pink splashes her cheeks. I shouldn't but . . . "How's the internet dating?"

A spark lights in her eyes, like she was hoping I'd ask.

"I made an account," she says, almost defiantly. "Last weekend."

I straighten.

"Really?"

"Really." She shrugs. "I surprised myself by doing it. But I figured I didn't have anything else to do. I'm not going to wait around, you know? People can't just think someone will make a move and never do it and wait forever." She lets that land; it does. "And you would never believe how eager the pool is. Trust me." Her eyebrows raise. "Very. Eager. Pictures and everything."

The hell? I could've sworn she was bluffing last weekend. Even in her texts I wasn't sure I actually believed she had other plans. But now? Now I'm not so sure.

"Really?" My eyes narrow. "Pictures?"

"Mhm." She traces a finger along a rubber mat on the bar. "Very well-endowed pictures at that. I didn't know dick pics could be so encouraging."

Her face fills with impressed shock. By pictures. Of stranger dick.

It takes all my effort not to growl like some kind of barbarian.

"How so?"

Her lips twitch.

"Show me yours, I'll show you mine," she says, lowering her voice and taking a step toward me. *Leaning.* "Know what I mean?"

Something is off. Her words mismatched with her mannerisms. She's not flushed or flustered. She's cool. Calculated, even. I stroke my mustache.

She toys with her hair.

"I have a date tonight with one of the men who liked on me. We're having a beer."

Liked on me?

"You're meeting one of them?" I ask, folding my arms over my chest. "Tonight?"

"I am." She flicks her hair over her shoulder with way too much gusto. There it is: She's lying. "I bought new panties—black thongs mostly." I happily visualize this now that I know she's not wearing them for someone else. "Very stringy. I figured, why not? What's it going to hurt? I've been out of the game a long time. This is a good place to start."

"Stringy?" I ask, dragging the word out. "Really?"

"Yes, *really*." A defensive edge creeps into her voice, and it's pinched the way it seems to get when I call her out. Judging by the way she keeps touching things behind the bar, she knows I know she's bullshitting me. "You think I'm just going to sit at home and twiddle my thumbs while everyone else is out having fun and getting sex?" She scoffs with a bat of her hand; I resist the urge to kiss her on the mouth. "I need the relief, you know? I need sex—now. I'm just a walking pressure cooker about to explode. Probably won't take much, really." She winces. "Probably just a touch." Another wince. "Or lick." Wince. "Or something."

I work my teeth over my bottom lip.

"You need to *get sex* now, huh?"

"Yes." Her eyes widen. "No. Not *now* now, like later now. On my date."

I press my lips into a flat line and she presses the back of her hand to her face—which is as red as the shirt on my back.

Headlights shine through the front windows as a couple cars park. The first guests are here. Too bad. This was entertaining.

I look her over one more time, visions of her with licks, touches, and black thongs dancing in my head. I am a grown man with a very big crush. "You'll have to let me know how that works out."

Her jaw drops.

I grin.

The door opens to usher in the rest of the night.

The tables and bar are filled with people, most of whom I've known for years and have supported the business since day one. The donation box at the door is overflowing with leashes, doggy toys, and boxes of treats as the band plays every Christmas song ever written with a twist of rock.

Goose, despite the chaos, doesn't budge from his spot on the floor.

While some people hate these things, I thrive on them. I love my job and the people who let me do it. Every handshake, conversation of beer, and wide smiled *Merry Christmas!* is genuine. My once *maybe someday* dream gets to be my daily reality. The scariest thing I've ever done with my life will forever be one of my best.

To her credit, Hollis recovers from her little act beautifully. She pours beer with focus like I've never seen and delivers plates of brats with a bright smile on her face.

It's only when she catches me looking at her does her demeanor falter.

I can't help but wonder what she thinks of all this. A night she'd usually spend at a bake sale with her kids, but instead she's pouring beer. Her smile looks genuine, but that doesn't mean she wouldn't still rather be doing what she's always done.

Behind the bar, I restock glasses as Hollis serves a regular, Rich, wearing his annual Christmas tree sweater with working lights.

"You new?" Rich asks as Hollis passes him a beer.

"Just helping for the night," she tells him. "You come every year?"

"Ain't Christmas without it. It's tradition," he says, taking a sip with an audible *ah!*

"Tradition," she repeats, like it's a new word in her vocabulary. Like she doesn't quite believe he's used it in the correct context. Like anything except her beloved town events can qualify as such a thing. Her eyes meet mine for a split second.

"That's right," Rich continues. "No place else I'd rather be tonight, right, Jay?"

"No matter how hard I try to keep you away, Rich," I say with a chuckle.

"Been coming here since Jay opened the place." Rich grins. "Best damn beer in the mountains."

Hollis doesn't hide her shock. "Opened it?"

Saw that coming.

I say nothing, letting the smile tugging at my lips do the talking as I wipe drink rings off the bar with a rag. Rich chuckles, oblivious, gesturing with his beer before returning to his table.

"Explains so much," she says, fighting a smile as she leans a hip against the bar next to me.

"Like?"

"The staff."

With a slight laugh, I drape the rag I've been using over the edge of the sink as the band starts a rendition of "Rockin' Around The Christmas Tree."

"Why didn't you tell me?" She regards the brewery again. "It's incredible."

I face her fully, mirroring her by leaning a hip against the bar. "You didn't ask."

She rolls her eyes but she's smiling. "Either way, it's nice."

"Thanks," I say, glancing around the familiar room again. "Took a lot of work." My brows lift. "And you were good tonight. You'll have to include beertending on your list of skills to your date."

I expect a laugh, but instead she levels me with a glare, abruptly moving away from me to scrub the bar I just cleaned then rearrange glasses until they look exactly the way they did when she started. When I think she's done, she drinks an entire glass of water.

"Is everything—"

"Fine," she snaps. She wipes her mouth and refills the glass, stilling it before it reaches her mouth when she catches me watching. "I'm thirsty because I'm distracted by my pending plans with the internet."

"Okay." So *this* is the game we're playing. "I didn't think you'd follow through."

"Why wouldn't I?" she demands. "A lot of people feel more comfortable with strangers on the internet. There's a name for it. I wrote an article about it once. It's called online disinhibition effect. People are emboldened by the anonymity of it. Acting emboldened. And doing things emboldenedly."

Judging by her grimace, that is not a word.

"And you're more comfortable with internet strangers?"

"Why wouldn't I be?"

"Well you don't know them and they're sending you dick pics."

"Maybe I like the pictures."

"Do you?"

She huffs. "Obviously, or I wouldn't be going out with someone."

I stroke my mustache. "Did you send them pictures back?"

Her eyes widen; I fight a laugh.

"No?" I feign deep consideration. "Maybe you should."

Her next leveling glare is a priceless work of art. "It's none of your damn business if I'm sending pictures."

"You should send them videos," I encourage.

"Videos?" she shouts, blue eyes widening before nearly closing as she gives an apologetic smile to a small group across the bar. To me, she angrily whispers, "Are you insane?"

"I'm just saying—" I push myself from the bar and start pouring another beer. "I'd appreciate a video." *Very much.*

She presses the back of a hand to her cheeks; I could have told her she's flushed.

"Don't do it, Hollis," Marv yells from the kitchen. "The internet is a one-stop shop to losing your identity."

"Noted," she shouts in response, squeezing her eyes closed before opening them with a sharp exhale. To me: "This conversation is over. I am fine. Thirsty and fine. I will not be telling my date about beertending because there's nothing to tell anyone."

I wave my palms like white flags. "Fine."

As I fall into brief conversation with a couple while pouring their beers, Hollis scrubs the glasses in a sink like they personally attacked her. She's muttering. She looks good—damn good—and judging by the caught phrase of *I should have never worn this stupid outfit* she's mad. At me.

I lean next to the sink, a *little* guilty. I should have let her have her fun. Should have gone along with the internet dating show.

"Listen," I say in a voice low enough only she can hear. "I—"

"No," she scowls, shutting off the sink with a slam. "You listen. I know what you're doing." Her voice is an angry whisper. "And you know what?"

"Hollis," I say calmly.

"You're right," she says over me. "I was never going to send a picture. Or online date. I, foolish as it is, am very attracted to you, Jay the brewery owner. I was trying to—" She drops her head back and groans, and all I can think about is how damn adorable she is and what her mouth tastes like. "To make you jealous by pretending I was."

"Hollis."

"It is purely seasonal psychosis making me act this way," she goes on. "And it's noted that you do not reciprocate, and you think toying with me is funny. Surprise: I'm an adult woman who swoons over hand holding." She laughs like it's not funny. "I invited myself to be your tagalong Holiday Club member, and that's all. I know you—"

"Hollis," I say a little louder and with a laugh, finally getting through to her. "Stop. Talking. I want to show you something." She snaps her mouth closed and I gesture for her to follow me to an empty adjacent room with one large window filling the wall. We stand at it, her eyes following the night-covered hedge of trees lining a driveway until they land on the lit-up clearing at the end.

She squints. "An Airstream?"

"I live there," I tell her. "With Goose. My dad was—is—a lawyer with his own firm. I worked there—with my brother and sister—as a lawyer—for years. Didn't love it—wanted to brew beer. I bought this property. Bought the Airstream. Built the brewery."

"A lawyer?" she asks, stunned, looking at me like she's seeing me for the first time.

Her reaction isn't unique. Most people think it's weird. Some people wonder if I couldn't hack it as an attorney and had to tuck tail to the woods; others think I'm too poor to afford a real house. When I made the decision, my sister was convinced I was having a midlife crisis, while my brother told me I had the right idea choosing a life of solitude. My parents, however, thought it was a phase I would outgrow.

The truth is, I like it. The simplicity. The ease.

"Real estate law, mostly. I wanted you to know." A hint of self-consciousness leaks into my voice. This woman bleeds all things tradition, so there's a good chance she won't appreciate this. Get it. Want to have any part of it. Judging by the look on her face, she's thinking those same things too.

She stares at the lit-up silver camper in the woods, chewing her lip. I wonder if she sees the chairs under the striped awning we could sit in sometime or the picnic table we could eat burgers at. Her silence lasts almost the entire time the band plays "Grandma Got Run Over by a Reindeer."

Finally, she says, "My kids asked me to bake cookies with them this week, and I almost told them no because I was mad at Ryan for everything he's done." She doesn't look away from the window as she talks. "I realized how stupid I was before I could. So, we baked the cookies—with store-bought dough—in the middle of the week. It was fun—even though I refused to turn on Christmas music. Then they told me they didn't go watch the movie in the park because their dad took them to see something different in the theater. It didn't bother me as much as I expected."

She pauses, seemingly lost in thought, both of us staring at the lit-up Airstream.

"Either way, this night every year, I'm usually with them at a table selling cookies, but I'm not. And the truth is—" She looks at me for the first time since she's started talking. "Tonight, I don't mind. Being here, I mean. I'm happy. Really happy. That I'm here with you instead of there with them. I'm not sure if that makes me a bad mom to say out loud, but there it is." Her eyes bounce between mine, not a drop of judgement in them.

"One day, I hope you invite me inside your home," she says. "And the next morning, I hope we have coffee under that awning in those two chairs." She points at said chairs out the window, scrunching her nose as she does. "At sunrise."

She smiles shyly, and without her even knowing it, plucks my heart right out of my chest.

"I'd like that." *Tonight.* "Mostly the part about the next morning."

She looks back to the window with a soft laugh. "You would focus on that."

A woman's abrasive cackle fills the air along with a man's deep voice.

"We should get back," I say with a reluctant lift of my chin.

"Yeah." She doesn't move, just looks at me. Just like she did at the drive-in when I held her hand in mine.

And . . . fuck it.

I take one step, wrap my hands around her face, and crush my mouth against hers.

She stills, softens, and grips my shirt with her fists.

Her lips part; I smile against her and swipe my tongue across her lips and tongue.

She moans.

"Rockin' Around the Christmas Tree" blasts through the speakers.

I slip my fingers into her hair; she tastes like my beer.

The kiss deepens; her hips press against me

A man's *Cheers!* echoes.

It's all tongues, teeth, and lips, kissing in the dark room.

At her slight whimper, I chuckle.

Suck her lip.

Pull away.

Peck her nose.

She wipes her mouth with the back of her hand. "Sorry," she says with a breathy laugh. "I didn't mean to."

I look at her and laugh, then peck her on the mouth again. "I kissed you, Hollis."

"Ha," she pants. "That was—that was—that."

My lips lift. "It was."

"Jay," someone shouts. "There you are."

I give a quick smile to the man calling to me from the doorway and gesture in the air with a finger for one more minute as she and I walk toward the crowd. She's flushed but different than usual. Not embarrassed: blissed.

As she starts toward the bar, I stop her with a hand on her arm.

"For what it's worth," I tell her. "The two minutes I believed you were online dating, I was jealous."

At this, she laughs, eyes bright. "Good."

Marv comes out of the kitchen—flannel shirt tucked into his sweatpants, hands on his hips, and a frown on his face that somehow isn't angry. He cocks an ear as if trying to decode a secret message in the fast-paced music that's pulling the partygoers to a small dance floor.

"Hollis." Marv says her name like it's an announcement. "We should dance."

A ridiculous smile overtakes her face as he marches toward her in his sandal-covered, socked feet.

I step behind the bar, and she looks at me.

"Go," I tell her with a lift of my chin. "It's a Holiday Club rite of passage."

With a grin, she does, and I can't help but watch. Hollis shimmies her shoulders and shakes her hips as she laughs while Marv's fists punch into the air with a washing-machine twist of his waist. The serious expression on his face as his head bobs is at complete odds to the playful atmosphere of the rest of the room.

I pour a beer, meeting her eyes across the room, feeling the smile on her face in every cell of my body.

Watching her laugh as she dances is like watching a sunrise on new snow. Better than any gift under any tree.

I drag my attention away from her long enough to talk with people at the bar coming and going. Friends of my parents. Regulars. A girl I went to high school with and her husband. When Hollis and Marv finish dancing, they slide onto two stools, and I set two beers in front of them.

"Tonight's payment," I say with a wink.

Marv offers Hollis a hot pepper.

She looks at him, me, the pepper, and surprises us all when she says, "I've been meaning to start putting hot peppers in my beer."

"Your life will never be the same," Marv promises, dropping peppers into each of their glasses.

She takes a sip and makes a disappointed face.

"It tastes like regular beer."

Marv grunts. "Government food has desensitized your taste buds, Hollis."

Hollis simply takes another sip.

"You know about Clyde Tombaugh?" Marv asks her. When she says she does not, he launches into a very thorough explanation—which I've heard multiple times—of who he is and why Pluto is still a planet in a place called Streator, Illinois.

I watch the whole conversation play out while I pour beers and say goodbyes. Marv is Marv—I appreciate that about him—but most people don't. Hollis, however, takes him in stride. Sees his weird and lets it go. Even as I watch her try to wrap her brain around why anyone would give a damn about the planet status of Pluto, she doesn't laugh—though I think she wants to—she listens. Like a fool, she even asks follow-up questions.

When the last guests leave, I join them for a beer—complete with a hot pepper—sitting right next to Hollis, my knee touching hers. At which she stares until her cheeks flush.

"But did we ever land on the moon, Marv?" I ask over the rim of my glass with a teasing wink to Hollis.

This sends Marv on his next tirade.

Hollis smiles and nods the whole time.

"You've done all these things every year?" she asks when Marv finally runs out of steam.

I chuckle. "There's been some trial and error."

"The errors have been Jays," Marv fills in. "One year he insisted on a bonfire and that almost burned the forest down."

Hollis's eyebrows raise.

"Because you insisted on using a torch," I defend. "And gasoline. And let's not forget the year you wanted us to go ice fishing, and the ice was so thin you fell in."

Marv's expression goes conspiratorial. "Notice the government-run park district did nothing to warn me about that either."

"And you think the government wanted you to drown?" Hollis asks.

Marv gives a wordless look that conveys how true he thinks this is.

"About next week," I say, changing the direction this is about to take. "It's Thanksgiving. Marv and I usually—"

"I can't be there," she says, expression crashing a bit as she mindlessly traces her index finger along the condensation of the glass of beer in front of her. "It's going to be too hard, you know? It's not just the meal. We usually get a tree—a real tree—and decorate it at night while we eat leftovers. Since I'm not getting one this year, I don't think I'll be much fun."

"You're going to be alone?" Marv and I exchange a look. "On Thanksgiving?"

I might not do things the way everyone else does, but this is insanity. Her? Alone? On a major holiday?

"I have stuff to do," she says. "Catch up with work. Clean. Online shop." She pauses before adding, "Record dirty videos of myself to not send to internet strangers."

If she's trying for a joke, she fails. Even Marv doesn't offer his two paranoid cents.

She's upset, it's all over her face. It's evident how much this matters to her and how hard it is.

"Either way," I say. "I'll send you the plans just in case."

She's silent a beat then surprises me by standing. "Well, thank you for tonight," she says with a tight smile. "This was fun. Really fun."

She walks behind the bar to grab her jacket and purse.

"Okay." My eyes narrow. Marv takes a long sip of his beer, eyes bouncing between her and me. "You going somewhere?"

"Yeah." She fumbles to get her coat on. "I should. It's late." To Marv: "Night, Marv. Thanks for the dancing."

He flicks her a salute as I stand and walk her to the door.

Outside on the small patio it's frigid; she's stunning.

And leaving.

"Why are you going?"

She laughs, adjusting her coat and retrieving her keys from her purse. "What else would I do?"

"Stay."

Her eyes narrow. "I can't stay."

"Why?"

"You haven't asked me out."

A laugh rumbles in my chest. "So that's what this is all about?"

"Of course it is," she says without heat, blue eyes bright under the strings of lights above us. "You said you've been thinking about it, and you haven't. I may invite myself into clubs, but I'm a woman of virtue, I don't invite myself on dates."

I hate that she's leaving, but I love the smile on her face.

"Maybe I will," I tell her, dragging knuckles across the line of her jaw before shoving my hands in the pockets of my jeans.

Even in the low lights, I see pink splash her cheeks.

"Maybe I'll say yes."

It hangs there. I could ask right now and she'd say yes. Instead I say nothing, her breaking the silence by saying, "Have a good Thanksgiving, Jay."

I nod.

She leaves.

Then I stand in the parking lot, staring until she's gone and wishing she wasn't.

A Cookie Confession
By: Hollis Hartwell

I want to start this by saying, I have never knowingly lied to you. In my years of writing in my personal blog followed by the years I've had here at *We Women*, I've prided myself on sharing my honest feelings and experiences—for better or worse—as I navigate motherhood. My humanity is what I believe to be the foundation of the connected community we have created. At least that's what I tell myself when I share my hard truths and some of you share yours in heartfelt emails. We are strangers who have found a common bond in our flaws and the path we are stumbling along.

Because of this precedence and the promise I made to you when I embarked on this seemingly lost season, I had a jarring revelation over the weekend, which I feel is my duty to share with you. I, Hollis Hartwell, might hate the annual Christmas bake sale, and I'm happy I didn't have to go this year.

If you were sitting next to me, you would be witnessing me covering my face with my hands and hearing my groan of despair at my newfound knowledge of this information.

For nine years I have taken part in the bake sale. I've dedicated entire days to baking cookies, many of which lead to recipes I've shared with you, as well as an entire night every year sitting at the table with my kids and selling our goods. I have always thought I loved this. Thought it was where I thrived. Our table is always perfectly arranged with cellophane-wrapped cookies, a brightly printed gingerbread man–covered tablecloth, and strand of battery-operated lights lining its edge.

I was so sure I loved it right until this very year when it wasn't required of me to do any of it. In fact, this year's requirement was for me to *not* do it.

I was devastated about all I was missing until I realized I was relieved.

It couldn't have always been this way. I know it wasn't. I made one simple recipe our first years—basic chocolate chip—but somewhere between there and here, I entered into a competition with myself, compelling me to make every cookie bigger, frostier, and fancier than the last. I didn't realize how bad it had gotten until this year when my kids told me they hadn't made cookies with their dad, and we had to make everything last minute. Short on time, we used premade dough. It was the most fun we've had baking together in years.

There was no pressure.

No insane ingredients nobody wanted to eat or candy thermometers bobbing in pans on the stove while the mixer mixed the next batch of dough.

We baked in the most basic sense of the word, and it was incredible.

Then, while my kids sat behind the table selling our shortcut cookies in the school gym, I was with my holiday companions for this year, at a brewery serving beer and smiling. I got dressed in clothes a far cry from the Christmas sweater I'd usually wear and spent the evening with a crowd a far cry from the cookie consumers across town where I'd usually be.

I loved it.

I loved getting to skip the event that has unknowingly become more of a source of stress than a celebration. More of a *we have to get all this done!* instead of *I wish this would never end!*

My holiday companions call beer and brats and dog bones in a box tradition, and I'll admit, I see the appeal. How the ease at which smiles came and went felt freeing and fun and almost too good to be true.

The entire drive home, my thoughts volleyed between wanting to believe the holidays could be so simple and refusing to acknowledge it as even an option. I warred with myself between wanting to be a permanent fixture in that brewery every single year and knowing the seasonally responsible thing to do is to force myself to make the cookies and return to my spot in the gym next year. The gym, no doubt, will forever seem darker and duller than the evening I just experienced.

I don't like the holiday bake sale, and I have no idea what that means.

Thanksgiving
Hollis

Jay
Potluck at my place tomorrow?

Marv
ghi ghatuvde ptudefdefghimn

Jay
Gross. Hollis, you change your mind?

                            Hollis
        As enticing as your "gross" sounds, I'll pass.

Jay
What are you doing instead?

                            Hollis
        No plans. Cleaning the house. Reading a book.

Jay
You should take pictures.

Hollis
Ignoring you.

Jay
Just saying . . .

Marv
pqrstghijkljkl ghdepqrde

～

When I woke up this morning, I stared at the ceiling until long after the sun came up, waiting for tears that never came. I called my parents who asked me repeatedly to make the short drive to Charlotte to spend Thanksgiving at their house; I declined.

Quiet and alone, I had my coffee from the comfort of a hot bubble bath, my mind moving in a million different directions.

Yesterday, the kids and I had breakfast for dinner before I drove them to Ryan's house. I used an entire loaf of bread for French toast and let them pour their own syrup, something I never do.

With a mouthful of food, Ava said, *"I wish we could have this for Thanksgiving instead of turkey."*

It struck something deep inside of me. Something so insanely simple I've been blind to: We could. I plan the meal; it could be French toast.

"Maybe next year we can," I said nonchalantly.

Every single person at the table went still, including me.

"No turkey?" Owen asked, swallowing his food. *"Or stuffing?"*

"If you'd rather have French toast." I shrugged. *"No. Or we can make something else. Everyone's favorite foods even."*

Their eyes lit up, mine filled with unexpected tears. It

wasn't sadness over them not wanting the same menu as always, it was delight. I was happy to see them excited. With me.

Jack shoveled another forkful of food into his mouth, oblivious to my emotion, and said, *"Let's have pizza. I can't wait."*

"Me neither." I had to swallow around the turkey-sized lump in my throat.

Maybe it's the season, Jay, or simply having all this time alone to reflect, but there's a shift happening. The way a snowball grows when it's rolled across the winter-cloaked earth, so too is something deep within me. Expanding. Morphing. Changing.

If I hadn't dropped them off with Ryan last night, I would have made French toast and pizza today. But if I hadn't dropped them off with Ryan last night, I never would have known it was an option.

Today, here I am without our usual turkey or chaos, but somehow, also without tears. It's Thanksgiving, but it isn't. I'm okay. Alone, but okay.

Jay texted his usual Holiday Club invitation last night, but it's been nothing else. After the kiss, I hoped for a call—a house call, if I'm honest—but true to him, nothing outside of our group text. Since his current move is no move, the last five days I've been swimming in replayed memories of his mustache-covered mouth on mine. What it would be like if it happens again. How far it could go. What he looks like naked.

And then I overheat.

But more than that, I just want his company. His compliments hidden in callouts. His thoughtfulness. The way he listens. His entire life story of how he went from lawyer to beer brewer.

I'll wait; I have nothing but time.

At three thirty, I pour my first glass of wine.

At four, I pour my second.

At five, I'm tipsy enough I convince myself to put on the blue lingerie I bought myself last week during my blatantly obvious make-Jay-jealous makeover.

Now, with soft Christmas jazz playing through the speaker and the fading glow of sunset spilling through the window, I'm staring at scraps of blue lace that cover very little of my skin in my reflection in the mirror.

Looking down the barrel of forty, my body hasn't completely jumped ship. I eat the seemingly million grams of protein a woman my age is expected to consume and march around with my weighted vest like every other midlife militant fighting against the effects of time. Any extra weight I carried since my last pregnancy melted off—for better or worse—in the stress of the divorce.

I angle my head at my reflection, spin to the side. Hips, ass, and side boob all in plain view. Without overthinking, I grab my makeup bag. I have one tube of red lipstick. I use it. Along with a thick cat-eyed line of eyeliner and three coats of mascara.

"What are you doing, Hollis?" I whisper to myself, biting my lip as I run my fingers through my newly highlighted hair to make it look like sex.

I wonder if Jay would like how this looks. Wonder what he would look like if I was underneath him.

Or him underneath me.

Another slow twirl, and I decide I'm either sexy as hell or drunk as a skunk. I laugh—loud and long. This is utterly ridiculous. Wineglass in hand overhead, I sway my hips, watching my mostly-naked self in the mirror. All I can think: I'd do me.

It could be the wine, my curiosity, or the fact a week later I still taste Jay on my tongue, but what if I sent him a picture? Or a video?

I go still as a statue at the notion, my mind doing a mental tug-of-war between thinking this is the best idea I've ever had or the absolute worst.

He point-blank said he'd like one. He was joking. *Was he joking?*

He was.

Maybe.

I take a big enough sip of wine it burns my throat before warming my belly like a hot spring of liquid courage. I don't think; I prop my phone against the lamp of the nightstand and push the red button. Even alone—that simple action makes everything feel a bit charged. Filthy, even.

I swallow too many times then force myself to the edge of the bed. Seated. Eyes closed. Letting my mind and hands take over.

Jay's mouth on mine.

I drag my hand down my hip.

His big hands in my hair.

To my thigh. Higher.

"I've been waiting for this."

I bite my lip.

His mustache drags against my skin.

The music plays.

I lift his shirt over his head. Trace a line into his jeans.

One hand finds my breast, massaging.

I ache, everywhere.

His mouth is on me. His lips. His tongue.

One hand is at the scrap of fabric between my thighs.

"I can't wait to be inside you," he says, solid arms wrapping around me.

The first moan escapes my lips. As does Jay's name.

His voice is low, there's a sexy smirk. "I want to taste every inch of you, Hollis."

Working myself toward a peak, my hips rock against my own hand. My eyes lock with my own on the screen of my phone. Knees bent, bright red lips parted, and back arching off the bed. I barely recognize this woman.

His green eyes looking right at me. He fills me. Drives into me. Over. And. Over. And. Over.

It may be my hands, but all I see is him. I don't slow down. Don't stop saying his name.

I'm close.

Closer.

Closer.

Driving my fingers right into the doorbell ringing.

The doorbell ringing?

I freeze, stricken with fear, silent as I stop breathing. I look at the phone like it's responsible for whatever hallucination I'm having.

The doorbell rings—again. I did not imagine it and I fall off the bed with a *thud*.

Who in the hell?

Heart jumping in my throat, I crawl across the floor and frantically pound the screen of my phone to stop the video; it drops to the floor.

The doorbell rings—*again*—this time accompanied by a rapid fire of knocks and panic seizing my chest as my eyes dart around the room. I half expect to see the red flashing light of a hidden camera.

Another ring, more knocks, this time muffled voices calling my name are added in.

"Shit," I mutter, fumbling for a robe—the only one I have being ridiculously sheer white silk and mostly lace—and hustle to the stairs. My self-sex-covered fingers grip the robe tighter, and the damn doorbell rings again.

I feel caught. Like whoever is here knows what I was just doing and is impatiently waiting on my front porch to arrest me for being a dirty pervert.

At the door, I pause, take a deep breath, open it a crack, and cringe when I see bright green eyes, an amused smirk, and a head of tousled dark hair.

"Jay?" I ask, stunned. A fresh shot of exposed mortification washes over me as I widen the opening of the door. He's holding a box and foil-covered dish. Beside a tree. And Marv.

Who frowns, takes a long sniff, and says, "You reek of pheromones and look like a prostitute."

Oh dear God.

Heat crawls up my neck, and I pinch the opening of my robe. "Thank you, Marv."

I do not look at Jay.

"Jay was worried you'd starve," Marv says, looking past me into the house as he takes a flashlight out of his pocket, clicking it twice. "You're a sitting duck here. Mind if I look around?"

Marv doesn't wait for me to answer before stepping around me and inside, disappearing down the hall.

I clutch my robe.

Jay and I stand at the doorway, cold clouds around our faces. His jaw is slightly scruffy, his thermal very fitted. I want to lick him like a candy cane.

"You're wearing lingerie," he says, twitch of his mustache conveying how funny this is. How completely ridiculous. His eyes bounce all over me—my face, my sheer robe, my bare legs—and when they make it back to my face, they are so filled with amusement it's like he's watching a stand-up comedy show.

I squeeze my eyes shut. "I hate you."

"Still wearing lingerie."

"This?" I say through gritted teeth, looking down at myself and regretting the choice. Regretting my whole life. It's painfully obvious what's under the pitiful excuse for a robe. The dark blue lace lines are so prominent against the smooth white silk they might as well be ropes of neon. "This is nothing."

"Close to it." His eyebrows lift. "You think about the kiss?"

"What?" I choke, clutching my robe. *Only when I'm masturbating to the memory.* "No."

"I do," he admits with a wicked grin and smug rock on his heels. "Every night. Right now, even."

I can't breathe. I'm nearly naked and hot. On my porch. On Thanksgiving. With Jay.

A blustery breeze blows, and my nipples respond.

Jay notices.

I pray for Bruce Willis to show up and shoot me in the face. He does not.

"That sounds like a medical condition," I say, shifting my weight between my feet. Defensively: "And I'm not starving, thank you very much. I have a stocked pantry."

Marv yells something about proper ventilation from the kitchen; I ignore him.

"You look good," Jay says, cool demeanor at odds with his whitening knuckles around the box he's holding.

I lean against the doorframe for support, wrapping my hands around my throat. Another bone-chilling breeze blows by I barely feel.

He takes a step toward me. "Tell me why you're wearing it."

There's a challenging edge to his voice that makes my body purr.

"This—" I pause to clear my throat, and my hands slip

from my neck to grip the robe opening across my chest. "I bought this for myself." While thinking of you. *Nope.* "After a glass of wine, putting it on seemed like a good idea." And so did giving myself a Jaygasm to the tune of Christmas jazz. *Nope.* "Now, I wish it was flannel and had more fabric."

"What do you do when you wear it?" he asks, running his tongue across the edge of his teeth.

My eyes bug out of my head as my grip on the invisible fabric tightens.

"*Do?*" I choke. "I'm not *doing* anything. What is there to *do*? I'm alone, I can't do much alone, can I? I'd have to, I don't know, really have an active imagination for that to work. To make me wearing this alone be more than just looking." I swallow, nearly pass out. "I tried it on, it fits apparently." I laugh; it sounds like a strangled chicken. "And now, I'm going to take it off." I wince. *Where are you, Bruce Willis?*

"I see."

"No," I say, wrapping my robe as tight as it will go. "There's nothing to see. You don't see. What you see," I say with finality, "is what you get."

I . . . am a fucking idiot.

His lips twitch, and his eyes flare like he's read me like a large-print book. Like I fantasized the scent of him on me into fruition and he's picked up on it like a bloodhound.

Another breeze, and he drinks me in.

"Did you buy it before or after I kissed you?"

I start choking—literally choking—and he laughs, finally having mercy on me by saying, "Brought you these." He gestures with the box with a foil-covered plate he's holding before bending down and setting them just inside the door at my feet.

Hands on the box, he stays crouched, lifting his chin to lock eyes with mine. His face—directly in front of the spot I would like to rub against his entire body—fills with pure lust. His mercy is short-lived.

He releases the box.
Pops his jaw.
Wraps.
One.
Big.
Warm.
Hand.
Around.
My.
Calf.

When he stays that way, heat radiates from all five fingertips and slinks right up my legs and my breath stops.

Marv yells from inside about going into the attic; I do not respond because I do not give a rat's ass what he's doing.

Jay stands—slowly—dragging his palm up the inside of my leg. To my knee. My thigh. Stopping at the hem of my robe.

My pulse slams at the apex of my thighs.
He pulls his hand away—slowly.
Stands fully.
Leans in.
And whispers, "You've thought about the kiss."
I accidentally whimper.
Our eyes lock.
He.
Smirks.

"Ass," I say with a gasped choke, pressing the back of my hand to my face. "I don't know what you're talking about."

He raises his eyebrows, delivering a wordless *the hell you don't* look. "Either way, we got you a tree."

"A tree?" I parrot, forcing even breaths.

"A pear tree," he corrects, gesturing to the lollipop-shaped potted plant next to him on the porch. "You said you usually decorate a Christmas tree, and I thought since you weren't going to this year maybe you could do something else. Plant it with your kids when you're done." He shrugs. "A no-tradition tradition loophole?"

I stare at the tree, letting its meaning settle into my marrow as my hands drop to my sides, and the chest of my robe splays open. Adoration for him zips through me, swift and strong.

"That—" I clear my throat, willing my body to remain upright. "Might be the most thoughtful thing anyone has ever done for me."

A soft laugh puffs out of him, almost like he's relieved, and he smiles. "Good."

We stand in an awkward silence. I want him to come inside and stay all night. I want him to say, *I've been thinking of the kiss and you, and I want to do it again. And again.*

But it's not him who breaks the silence, it's Marv.

"Clean," he announces as he breezes past me and pockets the flashlight. "Safe to return home. Happy Thanksgiving, Hollis."

"Happy Thanksgiving, Marv," I call after his retreating back down the sidewalk. "Thank you for the gifts."

He responds with a lifted hand and without turning around.

I brave a look at Jay; there's a stupid smile on his face.

"We missed you today," he says, stroking his mustache. "But this might have been better." I snort a humiliated laugh. "Leftovers are on the plate—Marv made puffin he ordered from Iceland." His eyes widen to emphasize that. "And there's something in the box to go with the tree."

"Thank you for this," I say, trying to suppress the emotion that's currently pressing against bone in my chest. "And the tree."

He hesitates—*kiss me*—but simply smiles and strolls down the sidewalk. I stand watching until the box truck barrels out of sight. Disappointed and bursting all at once.

Inside, I open the box. It's filled with ornaments. Partridge ornaments.

My face splits with a smile. Jay the lawyer-turned-brewery-owner who lives in the woods in a camper might be good. Really, *really* good.

I run upstairs and grab my phone, and for the first time ever, I dial Jay's number.

"That didn't take long," he answers, and I hear his smile.

"I want to go out with you. To dinner." The words tumble out of my mouth like falling dominoes. "Then to your place. To one of those chairs sitting outside of your place."

Silence. My heart pounds.

"Jay?"

"I knew you were thinking about that kiss," he says, smug.

"Fine," I admit.

"In today's clothing of choice?"

I squeeze my eyes shut. Somehow: "Yes."

"My chair will be waiting for you next Saturday."

I pantomime a scream.

"Fine."

"Fine," he echoes, amused.

I'm still smiling at my phone after he's ended the call.

Then.

Alone, dressed in lingerie and giddy as a schoolgirl, I hang every single partridge on a pear tree along with a simple strand of white lights.

When my kids come home at the end of the weekend, they declare it the best tree we've ever had.

I agree.

The Beauty of the Pear Tree

By: Hollis Hartwell

I have always believed in times of emotional duress, the only goal should be to wallow in that pain, replaying the sad movie of my life over and over and over. And. Over.

Hollis, I would say, there's no space for happy when so much is wrong. And worse, should I feel the slightest tinge of joy in the midst of these hard times, guilt, that Grinch, would rear its ugly head. *How can you smile when you need to be sad? Do you even care?* When my heart breaks like hearts break, I proudly patch myself up with a Band-Aid made from mesh and let myself bleed out, purposefully stalling in my agony. Yet another tradition to put on my list.

And now: holidays. Is there anything which underscores all that we've lost—or never had to begin with—more than constant cheer? Any better reason to throw a blowout pity party than the time of year dubbed merry and bright?

Alone and in the thick of it—I entered Thanksgiving with this typical mindset. A day of feast and family with neither? I had bottles of water lined up in preparation to rehydrate from all the tears I would cry. No amount of new clothes, hairstyles, or nights out with strangers could fix the deluge of tears that would fall.

But they never came. Not one. As much as I hated not being with my kids or doing all the things we always do, I wasn't even sad. I, Hollis Hartwell, pity party extraordinaire, sought not just joy, but delight.

Even though I was alone.

Even though the day looked anything but traditional.

My happiness felt jarring. Confusing even. Like a single red bulb on a string of white lights. My happiness has no place here, yet here it is just the same.

Are we allowed to feel good while also harboring hurt? A few weeks ago, I would have said absolutely not. Not just on principle but out of the fact sheer agony was too powerful a force in my heart and soul.

But today?

Today my answer is an emphatic *yes*. We can find reasons to smile even after life has yanked the rug out from under us. Two things can be true: We are allowed to mourn one thing while we celebrate another. Be lost and found. Anticipate the touch of another's hands while also taking matters into our own.

We are women *and*.

Mothers *and*.

Hurting *and*.

I can tell you right now, I don't want to spend every Thanksgiving alone. I look forward to next year when the kitchen table is a disaster and the sink is overflowing with dirty dishes, but it's almost as if this tradition sabbatical was needed to force me to learn lessons I wouldn't have been able to otherwise. My kids will grow up and move away; one day they will spend holidays with other people. That used to make me sad—mourning a future that hasn't even arrived—but now I feel a sense of capability. I love being surrounded by people and food on the holidays, but now I know I can survive without them.

I can find joy in other ways.

And the jarring presence of joy has led me down a strange rabbit hole of looking for other things that end up in this season which seemingly make no sense. *Die Hard*, of course, but also the items listed in the familiar song of "The Twelve Days of Christmas," a song so seasonally symbolic yet utterly nonsensical. Milkmaids? Geese? Drummers? As strange as the listed items are—as seemingly un-Christmas—they work. Maybe not so different than my own joy in a sad time.

After dissecting it over and over, I took to the internet to learn more about the old English carol and why a true love is delivering these gifts, most specifically the pear tree. It blooms in the spring and bears fruit in the fall—what is it doing in Christmas? And more, what's its appeal to the partridge? To the lover who brings them?

After research, I found that there are many interpretations of this whimsical gift, but it seems all roads point to it being a symbol of nurturing relationships, generosity, and—wait for it—tradition. Maybe it's all of these things or maybe it's none of them, but I decided maybe the mystery of it being there adds to the appeal.

Maybe it's the beauty of the blossom when it's in its right time.

Maybe it's the flavor of the pear or the green of its leaves.

Or, maybe like a ray of sunshine in the midst of the storm, the beauty of the pear tree is, regardless of how little it makes sense, it simply suits the partridge.

Perfectly.

December 7th
Hollis

Jay
Hi.

Hollis
Hi. I don't see Marv's number.

Jay
I thought maybe we'd give him a break since you already said you wouldn't be near him with weapons.

Hollis
So you're texting me to say hi? How very un-Jay of you.

Jay
I can be un-Jay. And maybe I'm excited to see you tonight.

Hollis
Eager. It suits you. Does Jay the beertender wear his antler hat on dates?

Jay
There will be hats.

Hollis
I'm not sure how I feel about that sentence.

Jay
You should wear your Thanksgiving outfit, it will pair well with said hats.

Hollis
I'm cancelling tonight.

Jay
Cancelling is against the rules.

Hollis
Is it weird I miss Marv's ambiguous texts?

Jay
Marv has an appeal even I can't explain. Should I invite him on the date?

Hollis
Not if you want me to wear the Thanksgiving outfit.

∼

Marv with a gun is a line I won't cross, which is why I skipped today's Holiday Club meetup of squirrel hunting in exchange for sleeping in and freaking out.
  I'm going on a date.
  With Jay.
  Tonight.

When he picks me up, I pretend I didn't pack a duffle and toss it into his back seat. He looks at me, mustache twitching. "You planning on staying a while?"

"That," I say, voice pinched as I white knuckle the handle of the passenger door, "is because I'm a messy eater."

"What a coincidence," he says as he starts to drive, reaching across the center console and slipping his free hand around my thigh. "Me too."

It takes maximum effort to not react to his touch, that innuendo, nor the visual both have conjured up, which involves his face between my legs.

I'm so nervous through his recap of hunting with Marv, what I tell him about the week with my kids, and everything else we discuss on the drive, it's a mystery to me what is actually said. He might as well be speaking in Japanese. I haven't been on a first date in twenty years, and I've never brought an overnight bag on one. Ever.

What kind of slut are you, Hollis?

"We're here," Jay says as we park.

I look through the windshield. "Puddy's House of Pancakes and Oddities?"

He grins as we get out and stand at the door, bright retro lights of the sign lighting our faces. He looks exactly like himself—tattered jeans, frayed-edge jacket, tousled head of hair, and mustache trimmed to Jay-perfection—but hotter by at least nineteen degrees. Maybe it's the anticipation of what's yet to come or what line we're crossing by being at wherever we are just the two of us, but he's mouthwatering.

"I thought you might like to know what kind of place has oddities *and* pancake batter on hand," he says, bumping my shoulder with his. "A peddling paradox."

My words from the wagon ride.

I swoon; it's stupid.

"But before we go in—" He reaches into his coat and pulls out—*is that a poinsettia corsage?* "I got you something." At my confused look, he explains, "It's tradition. Every time I take you on our first official date, I get you a corsage. Didn't you know?"

As I bite my cheek to keep from smiling, he pinches his tongue between his lips and slips the ghastly corsage onto my wrist. The bright red flower and the flashy gold sprigs sticking out around it are absolutely hideous.

Again, I swoon; again, it's stupid.

"Have I told you I like traditions?" I ask with feigned surprise.

He strokes his mustache in mock contemplation. "I wondered if you might."

We both smile like we can't not, and he takes my hand in his, pulling me inside the restaurant.

It's cluttered chaos. True to its name, oddities are everywhere, shelves upon shelves lining every wall surrounding an open area filled with tables where a few people are eating. Polka Christmas music plays a little too loudly, and the whole place smells like pancakes and syrup. In every corner, Christmas trees covered in vintage ornaments are shoved. In between, there are cases of glass bottles, creepy dolls, nutcrackers, and snow globes. One entire section is dedicated to top hats. And fishing lures. And puppets.

"How did you find this place?" I whisper, clinging to his arm as a hostess wearing a top hat adorned with candy canes leads us to a table in the corner.

"I get my nieces and nephews their Christmas gifts from here every year," he says, sliding into the same side of the booth as me instead of across the table. My shoulders tense at the silliness of it. Like us sitting so close will translate to everyone thinking we're bragging about being here together. But when Jay looks at me playfully, the tension dissolves. Because it is silly, and we are here together, and dammit I love both of those things.

The atmosphere is like a Christmas-themed circus. It's utterly wild, makes absolutely no sense, and is completely perfect.

"What on earth do you buy here?"

He chuckles, eyeing the red paper lantern painted with gold bells hanging over our table. "Oddities and pancakes, of course."

I snort a laugh, perusing the menu. The waitress arrives and we both order pancakes, bacon, and hot chocolate.

When she's gone, I angle my position so I'm facing him in our singular booth, and he drapes an arm over the back. Every look, laugh, and touch reads like a big fat flirt.

"You like me," he says, fingering the hair around my face.

"Hm." I gesture with my corsage-adorned wrist. "You're the one showering me in gifts, I could say the same."

"I do like you," he says easily, eyes not leaving mine. "I really liked you on Thanksgiving."

I slap him on the arm making him grunt. "That," I say, flustered as the waitress delivers our hot chocolates, "was not what you think."

Jay pulls out a flask and pours whiskey into each of our mugs.

"I think a lot of things," he says, smiling wolfishly over the top of his mug. Hot chocolate clings to his mustache, and I reach out and wipe it with my thumb.

He grabs my hand at his face and kisses my palm.

It's sweet.

And.

I swoon, not even caring if it's stupid.

"So," he says, setting his mug down. "Hollis the Writer, you still missing parades and bazaars and bad movies this season?"

I fill my cheeks up with air then deflate them with a slow exhale as I consider this question.

Parade versus surprise tree farm. Movie in the park versus the drive-in. Bakesale versus beertending. The truth isn't a revelation: I haven't missed any of it. I've noticed it as I've reread every weekly article I've submitted to my editor these last weeks. The parades don't matter. Most of it doesn't. But the kids, that's an entirely different story.

"I miss my kids," I tell him honestly. "I really miss my kids. Everything else so far?" I shrug. "Looks a bit lackluster now that I'm removed from it." I stare at my mug of hot chocolate and trace the retro pattern of holly leaves on its side with my finger. "I don't know if they like any of the things we've ever done, now that I talk to them about it." I laugh softly, folding and unfolding my napkin on the table. "I don't know if I'd be saying any of that if I hadn't met you—and Marv—so thank you for that. It's been what I needed."

I brave a look at him, and his lips tug to one side.

"You're what I needed," he says with a playful nudge my way.

"Oh, really?" I tease. "How's that?"

The waitress brings our plates of pancakes and bacon and the biggest bottle of maple syrup I've ever seen.

"I needed," Jay says, not hesitating to pour syrup on both our plates, "to learn not everyone who likes *It's a Wonderful Life* is a complete moron."

"Ha. Ha," I say flatly as I take my first bite of pancakes. And—"Holy buttery goodness, Batman. Why are these so good?"

He makes an agreeing sound, smiling as he chews; there's syrup in his mustache.

"That thing on your lip is obnoxious," I tell him before my next bite.

He grins, says, "Might be, but you love it," and fills his mouth with more pancakes then moans.

And that is our date: Me with a corsage, him with a mustache, both of us laughing as we eat pancakes in an oddity shop with spiked hot chocolate.

We talk about everything—how he learned to brew beer in college with a DIY kit he got for Christmas one year. How my writing career started in high school where I wrote essays for hire for most of the football team. How he runs for fun and I find that news completely offensive. How the mustache came to be—a lost bet on a football game—and how he would miss it if it were gone.

He tells me about his sister, Caroline, and how when she drinks too much wine, she confesses that she and her husband, Ben, smoke pot out of their master bathroom window after the kids go to bed then proceed to have kinky sex.

About his younger brother, Brent, who sometimes tells his wife he's going to work out but really goes to Jay's camper and plunders his fridge for beer in an effort to escape his screaming kids.

About his parents who have gotten into pickleball.

"They sound great," I tell him. "Don't you miss them around the holidays?"

"They dole out this kind of crazy all year," he says with a wry grin.

"Do you think you'll—I don't know—ever want to have a Thanksgiving with them instead of Marv?" The way he talks about his family it's evident he loves them. Even not knowing them it's hard to believe this man sitting in front of me doesn't spend the biggest holidays of the year with them. "Or if you meet someone you want to be with—" His smile turns to something slightly more serious at what I'm implying. "Not me," I add quickly. "I'm not saying me, I'm saying anyone . . .

I'm saying—I don't know what I'm saying." I'm rambling like an idiot and screw my eyes shut. "Never mind."

He's quiet as I take a long sip of hot chocolate, and I wonder if I've overstepped.

He clears his throat. "If I meet someone who wants those things without changing anything else about me"—he shrugs—"I don't care where I eat Thanksgiving. But Marv is a nonnegotiable. You don't just quit that man."

And though I laugh, part of me wonders if there's something deeper there too. If he's with Marv because Marv has no one else. It adds a whole new layer to my admiration for him.

Before I can ask, he pivots the conversation to my kids.

We laugh, talk too loud, and take a picture with the waitress in her candy cane top hat while we toast our mugs like dorks.

And in between it all—he drops pecks of kisses on my hands and cheek, like commas in a sentence making me pause just briefly. Little gestures to remind me we're right here, right now. I thumb his mustache, he toys with my hair. Christmas polka music plays as we sit on the same side of a booth. All I can think: *Hollis Hartwell, this might be the most romantic thing that's ever happened in your life.*

When the food is gone, we browse all the shelves filled with oddities and leave with gifts. He buys six creepy dolls for his nieces and nephews; I get four outrageous top hats for my kids.

"Now what?" I ask as we load our bags into the back of his SUV.

He closes the door and walks around to the passenger side with me.

"I need to take care of Goose," he says, standing close to me as he tugs at the lapel of my peacoat. "At my place."

"Ahhh." My voice has a slight teasing lilt, but my body is

filled with full-blown desire. "I see. So we need to go back to *your place* just so we can take care of Goose?"

He nods, very seriously, pulling me closer to him until I slip my arms around his waist.

"Exactly. It will only take five minutes. Maybe ten. Depending on what Goose needs and what's in that bag of yours—twelve hours tops."

I laugh, and he does too. Then he kisses me, deep and slow like he did at the brewery. He tastes like hot chocolate and maple syrup and moves his mouth with sexy precision. Like every swipe of his tongue and scrape of his teeth is working toward something. Dessert after a dinner filled with it. We connect at the mouth but every nerve ending across my body starts thrumming with life.

When we pull apart, we go to his place.

∽

Jay's camper is a sight to behold: a large silver capsule with big windows and a patio area wrapped in colorful strands of Christmas lights. It belongs on a Christmas card with the line *Wish you were here!*

"Before we go inside," I say, my mouth going bone dry as his hand stills on the handle of the silver door. "I'm wondering how frequently you do this sort of thing?" His eyes meet mine and I tighten the belt of my coat. "Bring women home, I mean. I don't need exact numbers, just more to understand if this is what we are doing and then that's it or if, I don't know, we do it again. Or am I kicked out of the club. Or . . ." This is not going well. "You're a good-looking man. I would expect you find yourself in this situation." His lips tug to one side; I clear my throat. "I haven't had sex in nearly two years. I need to go into this—" I wave my finger back and forth between us. "*This,* knowing if this is for tonight or if it's maybe—" I pause. Swallow. "Longer?"

"What do you want?" he asks, taking my hand in his and angling his head to meet my eyes. "Do you want to come in here once and that's it?"

The man could be a bag of milk in bed and I'd still want to come back here.

I bite my lip. "A different option might be better."

"Good."

In my belly: butterflies.

He tugs the door open and Goose barks then pounces on him before darting outside. My attention is already all over the interior, touching every surface like I'm blind and it's Braille. Like if I don't feel it all beneath my fingertips, I'll never comprehend it. The walls are rounded toward the ceiling making it a bit like I imagine a submarine would be. It's new but vintage. A little retro farmhouse. To the immediate right, a sleek leather sofa under a window lined with Christmas lights and a small coffee table on a plaid printed rug. At one end on the floor, there's a doggy bed and a stand holding two dishes.

Jay closes the door once I'm fully inside, and I feel his eyes glued to me.

To my left, a little strip of kitchen cabinets lines one wall. A small sink, small stove, small bright red refrigerator, and a coffee pot. A single magnet pins a large family photo of what I assume to be Jay, his parents, and brother and sister with their families. On the wall above the kitchen counter, a row of four hooks, which hold mismatched mugs. Across from the cabinets, a small dinette table with bright red cushioned seats and a butcher-block tabletop—complete with a mini Christmas tree under a wall full of windows. Outside: a tree line and darkness.

Down a short hall, there are two closed doors.

Jay clears his throat. "So this is it."

I nod but say nothing, trying to absorb it all. This camper is a fraction of the size of my house, but it's incredible. Small, but incredible.

I look at him, he's—"Are you nervous?"

He stuffs one hand in his pocket, a little pink splashing his cheeks for the first time ever as he strokes his mustache with the other. It's utterly adorable. "I know it's different than you're used to. There's not a lot of room for four kids to—"

My eyes widen. "You've thought of my kids being here?"

"I've thought of you being here," he says, leaning a hip against the small kitchen counter and crossing his arms over his chest. "So, yeah, I've thought about what that would look like if you ever brought them. The table turns into a bed. So does the sofa."

Being a mom makes you weird because those unassuming words send a shot of desire straight through me and nearly melts off my panties.

I shrug out of my coat and hang it on a hook next to a flannel then slip my phone out of my pocket and set it on the counter.

"That," I say with a lift of my chin as I stand next to him, "is incredibly hot of you to think about."

He hooks a hand around my waist and drags me to him, kissing me on the mouth with an amused rumble in his chest. My body responds like a lit match to a dry Christmas tree: consumed.

He presses against me; I moan.

Then I feel him.

Hard.

Because he has a penis.

That I'm going to have sex with.

For the first time in nearly two years.

At once, desire turns to panic.

Because I'm freaking out and don't remember how to breathe.

Pulling away from the kiss, I fumble to pick my phone up from the counter.

His mouth turns to a confused frown. "What are you doing?"

"Finding that photo to send you," I explain, the words knocking into each other. "From the oddity shop. Or the pancake house. Puddy's." I'm typing and retyping my password to unlock the screen to no avail. "With the waitress. How do you think that works?" His eyes narrow. "The naming of the shop when you have two specialties? Whichever one makes the most money goes first?" I laugh like a deranged robot.

His eyes can't possibly get any wider, and I can't blame him. Even I don't know what I'm saying or doing.

Finally, the damn phone unlocks in my trembling hands. I can't think, so I pull the photo library up and shove the phone at Jay. He looks from it to me, baffled.

"You find the photo and send it to yourself. So we both have it. Is there a bathroom in here?"

He nods slowly, looking again from the phone to me. "First door."

I fumble with the door, closing it too hard once I get inside. It's small—a human-sized dollhouse. A toilet, single vanity, and shower stall with a glass door. I turn on the sink, grip the vanity, look in the mirror.

"What the hell are you doing, Hollis?" I whisper to my reflection.

I'm freaking out because this is real. I am in Jay's little house, and we both know we are about to get naked and naughty. I am not a prude, but two years of no practice is a bit intimidating. Especially following a marriage where my sexing was shitty enough my husband needed to get it elsewhere. *Can*

you forget how to have sex? Is it like riding a bike? Will I bleed like a virgin? OHMYGOD—was I supposed to bring a condom?
    I squeeze my eyes shut.
    Sure, I've had occasional bouts of self-experimenting—though none quite like what happened on Thanksgiving—but that's nothing compared to a real live man and a real live penis in my real live vagina.
    I can do this.
    I splash water on my face then turn off the sink.
    And then I hear it: my voice saying Jay's name. Over and over.
    I still. Its familiarity striking me like a bolt of lightning.
    No.
    I fling the door open and find Jay. Looking at my phone. Hearing my voice say his name. Because he's playing the video I recorded of myself and never sent on Thanksgiving.
    "No." My voice is so pinched and weak, it barely pulls Jay's gaze away from the phone.
    I can't move. My legs have grown mortified roots, preventing me from lunging toward him. I want to shatter my phone into pieces and take off into the woods never to be seen by another human being again, but all I can do is stand. I throw my face into my hands at the same time I hear the doorbell ring on my self-made phone porn and groan. Because Jay is seeing me, on Thanksgiving, in lingerie, mid-masturbation, while he is downstairs ringing my doorbell with partridges, a pear tree, and puffins on a plate on the porch.
    "Hollis the Writer," he coos, setting the phone down.
    Once again, I pray for Bruce Willis to come shoot me. When I hear Jay take two steps toward me, I know it's another prayer unanswered.
    He pries my hands away from my face and I brave a look at

him. Much to my chagrin, I have never seen a bigger smile in my life.

I don't need Christmas traditions, all I want is to die.

"I knew you were thinking of that kiss the same way I was," Jay says in a thick, low voice.

"It's not what you think." There is zero conviction in my voice. "I was drunk."

He chuckles, knowing damn well I'm lying. I moaned his name for God's sake. On video. Repeatedly.

"Hollis," he says, pinching my chin and forcing my gaze to his. "I want to take you back into my bedroom, you good with that?"

Even humiliated, my thighs squeeze. Because yes, that's exactly where I want to go.

I have no words, so I nod.

That's all he needs.

Mouth to mouth, we stumble the few steps to the other closed door: his bedroom. I'll take in what it looks like tomorrow, for now, my focus is on his mouth, hands, and everything he's hiding under these clothes.

I toe off my shoes.

Fumble with his belt.

Swear at the bottomless line of buttons on his flannel shirt.

He sits on the bed, pulling me between his thighs.

Slides my corsage off my wrist.

My sweater over my head.

And stares at me before kissing along my ribs as his fingers dip under the waist of my jeans, peeling them off me to reveal a black thong. He follows the lines with his touch and gaze, the heat in his eyes telling me he fully approves.

"You're even better than I imagined," he rasps, kissing my sternum as I stand between his denim-covered thighs, his magical mustache leaving a wake of want in its path across my skin.

"You've imagined me, huh?" My voice comes out husky as my head drops back. My fingers tangle into his hair. It's thick and soft and I resist the strong urge to nuzzle my face in it.

"Nothing near as good as that video," he murmurs between a trail of kisses across my stomach and the swells of my breasts.

I heat, but for once it's not embarrassment, it's white-hot desire. A building pressure swirls from the back of my eyes to the tips of my toes.

His hands slide up my back, remove my bra, then explore the rest of my body. His mouth doing the same, sucking his way down from my lips. Across my jaw, down my neck, devouring my nipples.

I've had four kids, my body is far from perfect, but the way Jay's hands are tracing the lines of my skin and his mouth is consuming me, I become a goddess being worshipped. Like I've never been more sexy or sexually capable than I am right now. Like he'll do whatever I want him to.

"I was thinking of your hands," I admit as he stands, his head nearly touching the low ceiling.

"My hands, huh?" he says, a little smug as he steps out of his jeans with my help. It's my turn to drink him in. He's solid and lean and quenches every thirst I've ever had.

This. Will. Be. Good.

"Your hands," I say, slipping mine into the waist of his briefs and sliding them down his thighs. When he's fully naked —and blatantly hard—I add, "And this."

He levels me with a look of pure lust and—without him even touching me where I want him to—I feel the building of an orgasm.

He kisses me.

I arch into his body.

He rocks his hips—once.

"Show me what you want me to do," he says, mouth against my jaw.

I pull back. I have never been forward in the bedroom. Never asked for what I want or thought of putting myself first with it. Ryan liked what he liked, and I never challenged it.

But this is different. *Jay* is different.

Eyes never leaving his, I trace his mustache with my thumb. Stilling, my thumb lingers on his lips.

He licks it, sucks, then nibbles the end with a sexy smirk.

It's the push I need.

I guide one of his hands between my legs where his fingers start working against the ever-soaking strip of fabric while the other begins exploring every other curve of my body. His mouth is on mine, possessing it with his.

We're on the bed; I'm on top.

I grind against his hand.

"In," I demand.

He grins and obliges, pushing my panties to the side before sending two fingers—deep.

I scream—loud.

When he slips his fingers out of me it's to slide my panties down my legs.

Kneeling above him and fully exposed, his eyes are all over me.

"I want you just like this," I tell him.

His eyes flare in approval, and he positions himself so he's fully seated with his back resting against the wall at the head of the bed. He reaches over to a nightstand without breaking our gaze, fumbling until he has a condom. Eyes staying locked with mine, he rips the foil wrapper open with his teeth and rolls it into place.

My mouth waters.

I crawl over him and hover above his lap with my shins next to his thighs.

My breath stills: *This is happening.*

"Ready?" he asks, gripping my hips.

I nod, and lower—slowly—eyes glued to his the whole time.

The stretch is severe. I tense. Pause. Take him fully.

When I whimper, he moans—we both do—then find our rhythm.

I grind against him; he grips my hips.

I drop my head back; his mouth is on my neck.

I near the edge of bliss; he bangs me toward it.

Forehead to forehead, it's all hard grinds and gritted teeth.

Hands roaming, mouths moving. Hungry and desperate for more of each other.

Grind, grind, grind, *gone.*

The orgasm I've been chasing slams into me like a sledgehammer sending a litany of whimpered swears dancing off my lips.

In my ear, Jay whispers, "You're so damn perfect, Hollis."

I can't see straight, let alone speak, so I say nothing as I come down from the high, blissed out and euphorically limp. All the while Jay never stops working.

He kisses my mouth, rolling us over so I'm on my back and he's between my thighs. There's no hesitating, he fills me—harder than I expect—and positions my bent knees to his biceps as his face lowers toward mine.

"This how you thought it would be?" he asks, low voiced as he drives in and out of me.

"Better," I say with a breathy laugh as I raise my face to kiss his, missing the first time from the rocking of our bodies. "This is better."

He smirks and doubles down. I don't count the thrusts,

the heartbeats, or the number of breaths later as he comes and brings me right along with him—again—but it happens with a hard slam, clenched teeth, and his magnificent body wracked with tension.

It is sublime ecstasy.

We lie in his bed, tangled in sheets and around each other, and he strokes my bare back as I prop my chin on his chest as both our hearts pound. The Christmas lights from outside glow through the window, mesmerizing me. Jay loves Christmas. Jay is good.

"What are you thinking, Hollis the Writer?" he asks, teasingly satisfied as he looks down at me from his pillow-propped chest.

"Hm." I drag a thumb across his ridiculous mustache, both of us smiling. "I'm wondering why you like Christmas the way you do?"

"Ah." He nibbles my thumb before pulling it away from his mouth and interlacing it with his. "I always loved Christmas. People are nicer. More reasons to have fun. Older I got, the more it felt like a competition of busyness. Rushing and to-do lists. Rolling eyes as they talked about all the parties and events they *had* to attend with a *just get through the holidays* mentality. And after I left the firm, it made things strained with my dad for a while." His fingers dance down my spine. "This will probably shock you, but being forty with a relationship status of 'had a girl he couldn't keep and lives in a camper' doesn't exactly lend itself to smooth sailing at large gatherings." I laugh softly, and he smiles. "Either way, when the time I loved started to feel like a chore, I met Marv. My holidays became better. Easier. More laughs and less *Thank God that's over.*"

"And the girl you didn't marry?" I ask.

"The girl I didn't marry didn't like all this. Said she fell in love with a lawyer with a house, not a brewer with a camper. After that"—he shrugs—"dating has been casual. Simple."

That word hangs between us—simple. That's not what I am. I have four kids.

"I admire you," I admit.

"Yeah?" he says, drawing lines on my back. "Why's that?"

I shrug against him, releasing my fingers from his and dancing them across his bare chest. "You just do what you want. You're, I don't know, brave in a way I've never been. Happy no matter what."

"Hm." He traces my eyebrows with his finger, mustache twitching. "Is this about the bake sales you've decided you hate?"

I still, blink, then bite back a smile as I slap his chest, making him grunt through a laugh. "You've been reading my articles."

"If I say yes?"

"You have." I prop myself up on my elbows as an amused expression overtakes Jay's face. "And?"

"And what?"

"And..." I'm instantly self-conscious. I know what I've written—every single one this season has mentioned our time together. I trace a figure eight on his chest. "What do you think?"

He grabs my hand with his, stopping my movements. "I think you're a beautiful writer."

No surprise, I swoon, pressing my nose against his chest to hide the giddy smile on my face.

"Of course," he says, causing me to look at him as he strokes his mustache. "My personal favorite was your analysis of the pear tree and reading about all the *joy* you experienced on Thanksgiving."

"Asshole." I poke him in the ribs making him mimic the motion, both of us laughing. "That was about something else."

"Uh-huh," he says. "I have video evidence now, Hollis. Marv's sniffer was onto something."

I let out an embarrassed giggle and start to pull away, but he holds me firm.

Laughter turns to a kiss turns to touches, mouths, and him sliding into me and me crying his name out all over again.

The next morning, with blankets wrapped around us like we wrap around each other, we sit in one chair under his awning, drinking my favorite cup of coffee to date.

'Tis the Season for Empty Squares
By: Hollis Hartwell

Call me an old-fashioned hag, but I love a good calendar. Not on my phone. Not on a computer. On paper. Filled with penned words, highlighted dates, and sticky flags. Tidy and list-laden, I carry it around in my purse like a badge of my adulthood. *Look at me,* it beckons. *I can show you birthday parties, soccer practices, and pap smears!*

Come every Christmas season, nothing is more satisfying than seeing every square filled with green and red ink to showcase all there is to do. It means I've made it. It means I'm living. Full calendar, full life. Full calendar, full heart. Full calendar, full time.

This year, my squares are anything but full. During the week it's been our usual hustle, but the weekends are empty squares. At first, they taunted me. *Look what a loser you are*, they said when I opened my calendar on Friday mornings. *Look how little you have.*

Now I find myself reveling in those empty squares. Looking forward to filling them with something a little slower, a little more spontaneous. Something that doesn't get written down because it's too busy happening. Because maybe the goodness of it can't fit into a box or be explained by words.

It's a simplicity I haven't experienced in over a decade, much less during a holiday season. It's not just traditions I've been chasing all these years; it's the need to be busy. To keep going and going and going like a middle-aged Energizer Bunny to prove my worth—my love for everyone—by doing everything under the damn sun.

It's scary to imagine a world where I don't work to fill our days up. Will my kids be upset? Will they be bored? Will they find me dull? Will they see how much I love them even if I don't take them to every parade that passes through town?

I've always believed that having a full schedule and an ironclad plan was what made magic happen. "Today we are doing this fun, festive thing!" were the magical words that could incite so much cheer. But there's also beauty in being able to ask, "What do you want to do today?" A special kind of merriment in sometimes being able to choose your own adventure, even at Christmas. Maybe especially then.

In a season stretching and shaping me in ways I've never imagined, I'm daring to say more empty squares might be the key to more joy.

December 14th
Hollis

Jay
Bad news—the ice sculpting guy cut off a finger working on an ice yeti last weekend. We need something new.

Hollis
That's alarming.

Jay
Hi.

Hollis
Hi.

Jay
Is it weird I miss you?

Hollis
Only because we just got off the phone.

Jay
You're right, it's weird.

> **Hollis**
> You could come over here tomorrow. We could come up with a plan or I can show you my recording studio.

Marv
pjkldeapqrsde pqrstmnop

> **Hollis**
> Definitely didn't realize this was the group text. There is no recording studio.

Jay
Marv's traumatized me enough, he deserves it. We'll come to your house tomorrow morning and come up with a plan.

Marv
wdeapqr abcjklmnotghdepqrs

Jay
Or don't.

> **Hollis**
> I still don't understand.

∽

Owen, Millie, Ava, and Jack are currently having a staring contest in the kitchen with Jay and Marv.

Because Ryan got called into work and dropped them off without warning.

Because the ice sculpting competition The Holiday Club was attending got cancelled, and we were coming up with plan B.

Because this is my complicated life and I'm fully expecting

as soon as this staring contest is over, I will never see Jay nor Marv again. Then I will kill Ryan for thinking he can pull a stunt like this after he's the one who got exactly what he wanted by taking every weekend of the holidays.

Asshole.

Since the second the kids barreled into the house and saw Marv in his socked sandals and Jay in his flannel and antler-clad hat in their space, I haven't taken a full breath.

"Who are you?" Owen demands.

"Depends," Marv says, skeptical crease to his brow as he plants his hands on his hips. "Who are you?"

They all answer at once:

"We live here."

"That's our mom."

"I'm Ava."

"We're kids."

"You sure about that?" Jay asks with playful squint folding his arms over his *I'm with Santa* T-shirt. "You look like grownups to me."

At this, they preen.

I step between the opposing sides. "Guys, this is Jay and Marv, they are my—" I look at Jay, and he winks at me. For a split second I forget I'm in a room. Wearing clothes. With kids. And Marv. "Friends."

All four of them blink at the two men.

"And these are my kids. From oldest to youngest"—I tap each of them on their heads as I call them out—"Owen. Millie. Ava. Jack."

Jay steps down the line to shake each one of their hands. "Your mom has told us a lot about you."

That simple line paired with the ridiculous hat on his head causes them to visibly warm up to him. As do I. More than I already am.

"We've been doing things on the weekends you've been with your dad," I explain. "What we were doing today got cancelled and we were coming up with a new plan when you walked in. But now that you're here"—I flick my eyes to Jay—"they'll probably be going."

While Marv's eyes stay suspiciously glued to the kids, Jay's are on mine.

As happy as I am to see my kids, I hate the thought of him leaving. The week was pure chaos—his with work, mine combined with last week of school busyness of classroom parties, gift exchanges, and final tests. We haven't seen each other since last weekend. We've talked every night, but I've been looking forward to today—to time with them then being alone with him.

I've missed him. Since last weekend, I've only thought of last weekend. Being in his camper. His bed. His arms.

When he showed up this morning with Marv, my first thought was to eat his face with a kiss but didn't want to come on too strong, so—like a moron—I shook both of their hands.

"Jay already told me you've fornicated," Marv had said with a flat tone. *"And I'm an expert at reading body language. Your fake handshake needs practice."*

Jay pecked me on the cheek and whispered a raspy good morning in my ear.

And then, the kids arrived.

"What do you usually do this weekend?" Jay asks them casually.

"*The Nutcracker*," Owen says with a very on brand eleven-year-old groan.

Jay chuckles. "Not a fan, eh?"

"Ballet is for girls." My eyebrows pinch; Owen notices. "Sorry, Mom."

Another tradition down.

"It's fine." I wave a dismissive hand. "And I don't have tickets anyway, so you're safe from the ballet." A wave of celebratory sounds follow, which briefly annoy me. "But we'll do something else. Come up with a plan."

Jay leans over and whispers in Marv's ear behind a cupped hand. Marv grunts. Twice.

"If you four tiny humans can keep a secret, I'll show you the back of my truck."

From anyone else, that line would be incredibly unsettling, but when said tiny humans look at me for approval, I nod and they trot after him.

"I'm sorry," I say in a jumbled rush to Jay as soon as the door closes. "I didn't know. He didn't call. I—"

He kisses my mouth to shut me up. "You're a mom of four kids, Hollis. Don't apologize."

I search his face for any sign of a lie but find none. He means it. I kiss him again and it doesn't last nearly long enough.

"I've missed you," I admit. "This makes things, I don't know, not what I want."

He chuckles, and tucks my hair behind my ears. "That's life. We'll leave if you want. We'll stay if you want."

I bite my lip. I don't know what Jay and I are, but I know I don't want him to leave. Not that I'm testing him, but I want to see him with the kids. Four kids is a lot of kids, that has to be intimidating. Hell, I made them and half the time I'm intimidated by all of them. He has to see how unsimple this is to really know what this would look like.

"Stay," I hear myself say, kissing him lightly again. "But I don't know what we are, and I've never introduced them to a man who's, you know, a man." His mustache twitches. "I can't be the way I want to be, I guess is what I'm saying."

He leans in, scraping his mustache along the curve of my ear, whispering, "And what way do you want to be?"

"Naked," I admit easily and with a smile on my face.

He laughs, kisses me once more, and steps away, adjusting his ridiculous antler-covered hat. "So we'll keep our clothes on and I'll follow your lead."

Before I can say anything else, the door swings open and the kids appear, arms filled with food.

Food?

"That truck is awesome," Millie cries, delighted.

"It's like a whole grocery store," adds Jack, impressed.

Marv comes in last. "We have everything needed to make gingerbread structures. Hollis"—he tosses me a bag of powdered sugar—"make icing. Tiny humans"—he looks at the kids—"sort the supplies. Jay." Jay lifts his chin. "We need music and beer."

Then, like it was the plan all along, we make gingerbread *structures* from supplies Marv keeps in the back of his truck for God knows why. For the first time this year, loud Christmas music blares through the house, and Jay doles out three beers.

Jay is great with the kids. He makes a house—it's awful—and asks them questions. Favorite colors, favorite movies, favorite dinosaurs.

"What about Christmas tradition?" he asks as he lines the roof of his dilapidated shack with gumdrops. "What's your favorite one?"

"Mom wakes us up at 12:01 a.m. to see if Santa came and open presents," Owen says, tongue pinched between his teeth as he focuses on placing M&Ms in a straight line. "And she makes midnight hot chocolate."

The rest of them chime in with an echoed, "Same."

I smile at their smiles, but I wouldn't call it a tradition because it started accidentally. Five years ago, Jack was a baby and cried all night on his first Christmas Eve, finally waking the whole house up at midnight. There was no getting everyone back to sleep when they saw the presents, so they gathered around the tree while I made hot chocolate.

Even though Jack didn't cry any more Christmas Eves, somehow we kept doing it. Kept waking up at midnight to open presents and drink hot chocolates.

"I like after the movie in the park, we get pie for dinner," Millie pipes in. "With whipped cream."

"We do not do that every year," I argue through an incredulous laugh, recalling the few times we've done that as I scrape icing into a new bag.

Millie nods her head. "We do"—her siblings murmur in agreement—"because the movie always runs late, and the pie stand is the only one left."

"We've done it the last three years," Owen reports.

I step to the table, stilling a fresh bag of icing mid-pass to Marv. My eyes narrow. "That's not a tradition, that's a food shortage."

They laugh.

"I like when we say Thanksgiving rhymes." Ava gives her two cents with another *not* tradition that we've only done once. "When we wash the dishes?" She looks at me with a smile. I nod with a grin; we did that last year. "And say funny things about the food."

"Turkey Durkey does a hurkey," I recite, earning a chuckle.

Jay hooks his gaze with mine but says to them, "Sounds like a good mom."

And there—despite years of hauling four little asses all over town to sit through shows, contests, and parks, it's accidental pie dinners, midnight hot chocolates, and half-delirium fueled poems that they remember. Emotion clogs my throat as I watch them all work with little hands around the table. The remaining icicles of the season that have clung to me melting away. This, right here, despite my best efforts to run from it and hide from it and prove some kind of point of what the holidays are and aren't, feels like Christmas.

"Hollis," Marv demands. "Icing."

I hand him the full bag I forgot I was holding, eyeing his creation. A rectangular building in the middle is surrounded by a perimeter of gingerbread walls. And what appears to be a satellite dish made out of pretzels. And a candy-covered spaceship.

"Did you make a prison?" I ask with a laugh.

"Christmas compound," he responds without looking away from it. "The walls keep the government out and can detect flying objects from as far away as the moon. Trust me, it's possible."

This makes the kids squeal with delight and unleash an assault of questions on him: "Is it real?" *I'm not at liberty to say.* "Can Santa get in?" *Depends on his intentions.* "Where do they get food?" *From an underground greenhouse with solar sun lights.* "Do they have TV?" *TV makes you stupid.* "Why is your shirt tucked in your sweatpants?" *Speed.* "Why do you have all that food in the back of your truck?" *Only the ignorant trust the government with their food supply.* "What kind of name is Marv?" *A fake one.*

It's pure gold.

I work on my own house across from Jay, and his foot finds mine under the table. I smile at my gingerbread house like it's the most amazing thing I've ever laid eyes on.

"I like your hat," Ava tells Jay in her seven-year-old voice from next to him. "You look like you work at the North Pole."

Jay smiles, taking it off his head to set it on hers and flicking a jingle bell. "Looks better on you."

She beams; my chest tightens. Because as sweet as it is, he

can't make these kids love him right out of the gate—I don't even know what we are. If we're seeing each other after the holidays. If this is all too much for him.

"You don't have to do that," I tell him.

"I want to," he says. "She likes it."

He winks at Ava; she giggles.

"But you don't have to," I insist. "Because I get it. It's nice, but you don't have to."

He props his elbows on the table on either side of his house and interlaces his fingers, rubbing his mustache against a knuckle as he looks at me.

"Get what?"

Damn him for latching on to my words.

I huff a breath at the token smirk on his lips. "Get that we are a lot of people in one house and you"—I look at Ava, considering my words carefully—"might have other plans next year."

"I was planning on doing this again next year, actually." He cuts his eyes to Ava and scrunches his nose as he leans toward her slightly. "If Ava will have me, that is."

He means it. She giggles. I swoon.

"Do you like my mom?" Ava asks him, making me choke.

"Ava," I scold in a whisper, stilling my icing bag mid-squeeze. "That's not polite."

"If I do like your mom," Jay says, ignoring me, "would that be okay with you?"

She nods, smiling wide.

Jay flicks his gaze to me, working a playful tongue over his bottom lip as he leans toward her and asks with a stage whisper, "You think she likes me back?"

"Yep." Ava looks at me and my face heats. "She's smiling a lot."

He gives me a smug look, but to her he says, "That's good info. I need someone on my side."

I press my lips between my teeth, lips begging to split with a smile. They both get back to work on their gingerbread houses like he didn't just say *that*.

Mariah Carey's voice sends "All I Want for Christmas is You" blasting through the speaker, and Marv says something about aliens that makes the kids laugh. Under the table, I play footsie with a man I like a little more now than I did this morning.

This isn't the day I hoped for, it's better.

What Is a Tradition?
By: Hollis Hartwell

We are mere weeks from Christmas in a year I have done my best to resist all my usual traditions of the season, big and small. I haven't been to any festivals, made my Christmas tree–shaped pancakes, gone caroling around the neighborhood, or sent a family Christmas card of all of us in matching sweaters. I haven't forced my kids to put their hands in another plate of plaster of Paris so I can preserve yet another year of the size of their little fingers and palms to hang on the Christmas tree (which I also didn't go to a tree farm and chop down).

Yet as I sit here writing this, I find myself happy. Happier than I've been in recent history, if I'm honest. And deeply troubled. How can I be happy in the midst of a season I love without the traditions I've clung to for a lifetime and the kids I love more than my own life? How am I sitting at my computer with a smile on my face writing nothing about what I've written about for the last decade of my life?

In a season I love because of everything the season represents, here I sit loving it anyway without any of that in the traditional sense. I don't have my kids on the days I want them most, but I've found joy in spending those days with other people. My home is devoid of any usual décor, yet when I wake up in the morning, I wonder if Santa came early.

For the first time this season, over the weekend, my unexpected holiday companions of the year had a run in with my four children. I thought for sure this collision of my two seasonal worlds would be the end of something I don't have a name for but also don't want to let go of. Like every surprise I've gotten on this gumdrop-lined path I've been travelling, it felt like anything but the end.

Not only did we sit and make gingerbread creations out of a random and makeshift supply of groceries, but the kids had fun—I dare say we all did—even though the gingerbread houses were mostly terrible and nowhere close to traditional.

But it wasn't what we did that had my heart clattering like the hooves of reindeer on a rooftop, it was something my kids said. When listing off their favorite things we do together each year, they didn't list anything big or showy. There weren't any plays, parades, or picture-perfect moments that topped their favorite memory lists. It was little things that happened in between everything else. Quiet moments filled with laughter or eleventh-hour belly grumbles leading to poor nutritional decisions but happy faces. They weren't traditions at all.

Or were they?

As these moments have had a pesky habit of doing to me this Christmas, I dwelled on these thoughts all night, wondering what I've been doing it all for. Am I chasing memories for my kids or doing things because I love them? And even more, if I haven't missed any of our usual traditions and my kids haven't missed them, what—and who—are they all for?

In the middle of the night, I pulled out a dictionary and looked up the word tradition. By definition, it means *an inherited, established, or customary pattern of thought, action, or behavior*. I read it so many times the word stopped holding meaning, only leaving me more confused and frustrated than ever. Like I've unwrapped a present only to find another layer of paper beneath it.

So here I sit, stumped but smiling, giddy to find out what's underneath that next layer of paper.

For better or worse, we'll find out what's there, together.

December 23rd
Hollis

The start of the school's winter break means the start of the kids being with Ryan for two whole weeks. I hate him for it, but not nearly as much as I would if I wasn't lying in Jay's bed.

Naked.

With him on top of me.

For the third night straight, he's bringing to life every little piece of me I thought died with my marriage.

Especially when he puts that blessed mustache of his between my thighs and doesn't stop working until he makes me see stars.

"Missed you," he says, as he drops his head in my lap, the only thing either of us wearing is a blanket.

Outside the window, snow falls for the second day turning the world around the camper into a winter wonderland.

I trace his mustache. "You went to the brewery for three hours. You can't miss me in that amount of time."

He rumbles with a laugh that vibrates my lap. "Looks like I can."

I hum an agreeing sound, moving my fingers from his mustache to his lips, him nibbling like he does before I move on to his jaw, then chest, then arms. All the way along him until our fingers interlace. I don't know if what's travelling between us is infatuation or intense fondness, but connected like this, whatever it is grows bigger within me.

"Christmas will be different for me next year," I tell him. "Life will be different. I'll have my kids more. This will be complicated."

"You will." His thumb swirls over mine. "I like your kids." He brings the back of my hand to his mouth and kisses it. "And at least one of them likes me."

"She's seven, give her time," I tease.

I look around his camper. It's so perfect . . . for him. I don't know how this works. What comes next. How we go from me and him hiding from the holidays in our own little snow globe to being me, him, and my four kids with the holidays and a whole life outside of them. It feels impossible. Like I'd ruin the good thing he has with boo-boos and bedtime routines. Like maybe this is all we can ever be.

"Hey," he says, sitting up so his eyes are level with mine. "You're upset."

I blink to fight ridiculous tears.

"Sorry." My voice is brittle. "I don't know why."

He kisses me gently. "I do."

I sniff. "Yeah?"

His lips press into a frown. "You're worried your kids like me more than you."

I laugh as I poke him, making him grunt; he pulls me into his lap and kisses my temple. "Tell me what's going on."

I sniff, wiping my eyes. "I don't know. I feel happy. And I like you. *Like you* like you." I ignore his smirk. "And I'm worried that you'll, I don't kn—" A ringing phone cuts me off.

My ringing phone.

I reach across Jay to the shelf to grab it, Ryan's name flashing across the screen making my pulse pick up its pace as I answer. He *never* calls. Something is wrong.

"Ryan?"

"Hollis. Hey." He clears his throat. "Listen. The kids are crying."

I straighten, pinching the blankets around me and gripping the phone tighter. "What do you mean crying? Is everything okay?"

Jay's eyes narrow.

"I mean—" Ryan blows out a sharp breath. "They want you for Christmas. Maybe I shouldn't have—" He cuts himself off. I can picture his annoyed expression and hand raking through his hair. "Maybe this schedule isn't what's best."

I've fully stood from the bed, squeezing the blanket around my chest while my body starts to buzz with anticipation of his next words.

"What's best?" I repeat, needing him to say it.

Jay's standing now too, pulling his jeans up his legs, concern etching lines down his face.

"Look, I don't know what to say, Hollis," Ryan continues. "The kids want you for Christmas, and I'm saying I think it's best. They're upset. Something about special hot chocolate and matching pajamas. This was never my thing. I can drop them off first thing tomorrow. That work?"

An ornament-sized lump fills my throat.

"Yes," I manage. Before I hang up: "Ryan?" There's a brief silence. "Thank you."

We end the call before I scream so loud Jay jumps. I wrap my arms around his neck and press my mouth to his through an excited squeal.

"The kids are going to be home for Christmas," I tell him between kisses. "He's dropping them off tomorrow."

Jay chuckles. "Good."

"Good," I repeat, pressing my cheek on his chest as I absorb what this means. "Christmas Eve with them, Jay. I'll make spaghetti and we'll watch movies then at midnight—oh my God." I jerk away from him. "Tomorrow's Christmas Eve."

He lets out another chuckle as he rubs my back. "It is."

I drop my blanket and push away from him fully, searching for my clothes. Frantic.

"I don't have anything ready for them." My underwear is in the blankets; I hurry them up my thighs. "They can't just be home on Christmas Eve with no decorations." I snatch my jeans off the floor and shimmy into them. "I have to go." I skip the bra and grab my sweater. "I have to get ready."

Jay doesn't move, he merely watches me blow around him like a tornado. "You're leaving? It's late—what's there to do now?"

I guffaw. "Of course I'm leaving. I have to get ready. I have to-to-to do everything I haven't done for the last two months." I'm nearly shouting now, my mind reeling with everything that needs to be done. Do I have enough presents? I hadn't even considered Santa when I was shopping—that was on Ryan this year. Now it's on me.

Shit.

I make a mental grocery list. Marshmallows, cocoa, sugar—I bump into Jay and laugh as I kiss him on the cheek. "Can you believe this is happening?"

He's so calm right now, it's like he doesn't see how insane this is. Like he doesn't know how much work there is to be done.

"Let me help you," he offers, tugging a thermal shirt over his head.

God he's handsome.

I shake my head, grabbing my toothbrush from the bathroom, him following me. "No way, I wouldn't do that to you." Translation: Please come with me. But I know better. Relationships haven't worked for him because he wants life the way he wants it; I won't push that boundary. I refuse. Whether we have strong enough legs to walk after this season I don't know, but me forcing him into a wrapped box under a tree today won't be where it ends. "Enjoy Christmas Eve with Marv the way you always do. You don't want this chaos." I stop in the kitchen to peck him on the mouth. "You have a good thing here, Jay. I'm not going to be the one to bring it down." I chuckle, my thoughts pulling me in a million directions. When my eyes land on him again, he's uncharacteristically serious. Maybe even hurt. "What's wrong?"

He clears his throat and stuffs his hands in his jeans. "Nothing. Happy for you. I know this is what you wanted."

I kiss him again; something is off. "Right. Well tomorrow Holiday Club meets, I can't be there obviously, but you and Marv are going snowshoeing, right?"

He nods. I can almost feel him withdrawing. Because this is my life. Because kids make things less simple.

"Yeah." He swallows. "And Christmas—Marv planned something this year, I forget."

The energy of the entire camper shifts from ridiculously cheerful to terribly tense, but there's no time to dwell on it. I barely have time to put on a coat, grab my purse, and pet the dog on my way to the door.

"I'll call you," I tell Jay. "When I get everything figured out."

I kiss him one last time then open the door.

"Hollis," he calls from the doorway when I'm nearly at my

minivan. I turn and look. "I'm good with chaos." He shrugs. "Just so you know."

My eyes bounce from him to everything around him. The ground covered in snow and flurries still blowing through the air. Little piles of white stick to random crevices of the camper and the branches of bare trees like they've been coated in icing. I wish I could ask him to come with me. Wish Christmas meant him *and* them.

I smile but feel a pang of sadness.

"Of course you are," I say.

Then I'm gone, out his driveway and down the road, his beacon of Christmas in the woods disappearing as I go.

I replay his words the entire drive. At every red light and on every aisle in the grocery store.

It isn't until I hear them when I'm sitting under a partridge-covered pear tree wrapping gifts that I know what he meant.

CHRISTMAS EVE
JAY

Hollis
Merry Christmas, Holiday Club! Thanks for letting me tag along this year :)

Marv
abcghdeabcjk ajkljkl
dejkldeabctpqrmnomnghiabc
gghideftpqrs defmnopqr
tpqraabcjkghimng
ddetuvghiabcdepqrs

Hollis
Wait . . .Check all electronic gifts for tracking devices. I figured it out!

Jay
Took you long enough, Hollis the Writer. Enjoy today. I'm disappointed you'll miss Marv's snowshoeing outfit.

Hollis
Next time.

Jay
Next time.

～

The woman crying in the bowling alley wouldn't have been so problematic if I wasn't falling in love with her. That's how it goes though, right? Life gives you what you need when you least expect it.

I throw the tennis ball to Goose, and he barks before pouncing through the snow to retrieve it, stopping halfway back to where I'm standing to roll around in the white powder.

When Hollis left last night, I wanted her to take me with her. I wanted to help her do whatever it is she does on Christmas. Wake up at midnight and make hot chocolate—I love hot chocolate. I would have volunteered to play Santa for her four hilarious kids. But she didn't want me to. Even after I offered, she shot me down.

It's early with kids—we've only known each other two months and I've only met her kids once. I know these things take time. There's more to consider than just me wanting to be there. But I can't shake the thought that maybe she can't see me there. Maybe what we've been is all we'll ever be. Fun for a season. A distraction from what she didn't have.

Goose retrieves the ball, and I scrub him on the head before throwing it again.

I don't usually dwell on the comings and goings of women in my life, but she's been poking at every thought since she left. Distracting me.

Even Marv noticed this morning.

"*You've been infiltrated,*" he stated, somehow managing to keep a fur coat—which he made from an assortment of pelts he'd harvested—tucked into his sweatpants while his snowshoes crunched the snow of the trail. *"It was bound to happen."* I gave him a flat look but didn't argue—he probably has some gadget letting him know what was going on between us before I even knew. *"You aren't as strong as I am, Jay. Don't look so surprised. This is why I pay for sex. Strictly business. Carnal. Business."*

I let out an incredulous laugh and scrubbed the visual. *"Noted."*

A cardinal landed on a branch beside us, and Marv pivoted the conversation to a theory that birds were government drones. It was a welcomed distraction.

When we finished the hike, I made my rounds to see my family and deliver their gifts.

My mom gave me an annoyed look and her usual *I Don't Know Why You Can't Come Here For Christmas Breakfast, You Can Even Bring Your Strange Friend* lecture. I ignored the way that, for the first time in years, I kind of wanted to be part of the breakfast and laugh at the chaos over bottomless mimosas.

Brent told me he was jealous I wasn't putting a dollhouse together in the middle of the night. I smiled but didn't tell him part of me was jealous of him. Just because I don't have the kind of chaos he and Caroline have—the kind of chaos we grew up in—doesn't mean I don't love it.

As much as I love the path I'm on, part of the reason I was quick to pull away from holiday events five years ago was because it was a sore spot seeing them so easily have what I didn't. I left the stable career and normal house to live in the woods and brew beer—I knew it was no woman's fantasy when I made the choice. Sure, they lectured me, but I'm a big boy and could take it. It was easier not to be forced to see how chasing one dream took me away from another.

But it was my sister who sniffed out my bullshit this morning.

"You know you can live however the hell you want, right?" Caroline asked. "Dad doesn't even care you quit the firm anymore—I think he's jealous you got out early." I laughed at that, but she kept looking at me skeptically over the rim of her wineglass as we sat on the steps of her front porch.

I knew she wasn't wrong. When I left the firm, my dad was furious, they all kind of were. Like me leaving was a personal attack on them, though it was anything but. Years between the decision and now have made things better. Time has closed the gap between all of us. Caroline and Brent came around the fastest, as they were more worried about my sanity than concerned about my life being over. My dad was slower, but he came around. It's all water under the bridge. He drinks my beer, I laugh at the too-short shorts he wears playing pickleball. He's never said it outright, but at some point, I think he realized there's no one right path in this life, and he's accepted this is mine.

"Something's off about you," Caroline pushed. When I didn't respond, she squealed—literally squealed. "Oh my God, Jay. Have you met someone?"

She's like a bloodhound with these things, so there was no use denying it. I told her about Hollis—all of it. Her divorce, kids, and crazy stance on traditions.

"So what's the problem?" She set her wineglass down and pulled a joint and lighter from the pocket of her sweater, making me laugh once again as she lit it. "Go get this broad. I need more estrogen in my life. You and Brent are like cavemen."

"I'm not sure how," I admitted, taking a small hit of the joint when she offered it. "She's good, Car. Really good."

She frowned. "You're good too, Jay." She took one more hit of the joint before stubbing it out. "And it doesn't sound like she wants to change you like that last bitch you dated."

I laughed; she was right. Hollis, despite how different we

are on some things, seems completely fine with me the way I am. The Airstream. The brewery. Even Marv. After all this time with him, I'd never just be able to let him be alone on the holidays even if I wanted something different.

"*You're annoying,*" I told her as I started to leave. "*Merry Christmas anyway.*"

"*Go get her, Jay.*"

She said it like it was just that easy. Like I was Santa with magical reindeer and all I had to do was fly into the sky and land on her roof. Like she didn't have kids to consider and a whole life to get back to.

Before I could tell Caroline any of that, one of her kids screamed and she rolled her eyes before retreating into her house.

In all appearances, it's been a perfect Christmas Eve alone like the last years have been, only this time, I'm wishing I wasn't.

A blustery breeze blows across my face and burns my ears.

"Goose," I call.

He pounces toward me with a ball in his mouth and follows me into the Airstream where I poke at the roast in the crockpot then check my phone—again—to see that Hollis hasn't called—again.

After her text this morning, I was hoping to hear from her. Maybe even expecting it.

At the Christmas tree on the table, there are five gifts—Holiday Club bowling shirts for each of Hollis's kids and her. Which, since I'm down some self-loathing spiral, feels a little stupid of me. She might never call. If she doesn't that means she's made her mind up. On the other hand, women love to be pursued, so maybe I should call. And she's busy with four kids, she might have forgotten.

I rake a hand through my hair, stroke my mustache.

This is fucking stupid.

I check my phone again. I should just call. I will call. Tonight. When her kids are in bed. Or maybe at midnight. Or twelve thirty when I know they're awake.

I swipe my keys off the counter—I'm driving over there. If she doesn't want me to stay, she'll just tell me. I can handle that. I *think* I can handle that.

When I swing open the door, I still, my heart skipping several beats as I fight the smile pulling at my lips.

Hollis stands red nosed and smiling with a green beanie on her head and her face lit up from the glow of the lights hanging around her. Her fist hovers midair like she was about to knock.

"Jay," she says, sounding surprised that I'm here. "You're here."

"Looks that way." I lean against the doorframe, pinching my lips together. Under her usual black coat, she's wearing bright red-and-green striped pajamas. "As are you."

She laughs; it's nervous. "I—yes. I'm here and you're here." She's beautiful. "I'm—" She laughs again. "I've missed you."

"It's barely been a day," I say, stroking my mustache so I don't grab on to her. "You can't miss me."

She shrugs with a slight smirk. "Looks like I can."

I step down the two steps so I'm directly in front of her. "Looks like it." Over her shoulder, her minivan is still running, and four little faces are pressed against one window. I chuckle. "And you brought company."

"Right," she says, once again nervous. "About that. I realized when I left, maybe I didn't want to. Maybe you didn't want me to." She pauses, eyes searching mine. "And I thought, I didn't get this far by not inviting myself into places I didn't belong. So, maybe, if you'll have us, we can have Christmas here. With you. As a new tradition. Christmas Eve in an Airstream has a ring to it."

When she pauses again, adoration for her bends my bones.

"I brought food," she adds quickly. "And I don't want to impose. I know this is your time. And I talked to them about the space. To not touch anything without asking. We can also go home—if this is too much, I mean. I don't want you to think—"

I kiss her. Because I can't not as much as to shut her up. "Hollis," I say, keeping my mouth close to hers. "I want you here." She opens her mouth. "All of you."

She bites her lip but smiles around it. "We also brought you pajamas."

I chuckle. "Can't wait."

She turns and gives the kids two thumbs-up, and they barrel out of the van, boots on their feet, hats on their heads, and wearing the same pajamas as she is. Under their arms: sleeping bags. Goose pounces around me toward them, making them scream with delight.

Right on time, snow flurries start to fall from the dark Christmas Eve sky.

Marv's truck pulls up; I look at her.

"Also, I invited Marv," she explains. "Apparently he has a bed in the back of his truck, a generator to run a heater, and something called a composting toilet."

Marv emerges from his truck wearing a pelt hat on his head and holding a game strap of ducks. "Merry Christmas, tiny humans. I brought dinner."

No surprise, the kids scream.

I look at Hollis's heart-shaped face and full lips, kissing them again before running my fingers through the hair peeking out from the bottom of her hat. "I *like you* like you, Hollis the Writer."

She smiles and thumbs my mustache. "I *like you* like you, Jay the Beertender."

When the kids are done screaming and the bonfire over which we cook the ducks burns out, we cram into the Airstream like sardines in a cozy can. At midnight we drink hot chocolates while we watch the kids open presents and litter the camper with wrapping paper.

And the next morning, we wake up early, all wearing matching pajamas, and surprise my family by joining them for breakfast at my parent's house . . . with Marv.

It's the best season for The Holiday Club yet.

The Gifts We Get Instead

By: Hollis Hartwell

When I was eight, I wanted a bike for Christmas. Not just any bike: a Princess Sparkle Unicorncycle. It had a hot-pink frame I could put my Lisa Frank stickers on, silver sparkly tassels coming out of the handlebars that would flutter in the breeze, and, perhaps the best part, a unicorn horn sticking right out of the front and a rainbow tail sticking right out of the seat. Advertisements showed little girls in fantastical (albeit impractical) gowns speeding down the sidewalk with big smiles on their faces and tails flying in the wind. That bike consumed my every waking thought. It was all I wrote about for my school assignments and all I doodled on scrap pieces of paper. That bike wasn't just gorgeous, it represented a special kind of freedom that only a child could understand. Did I mention the unicorn horn *and* tail?

Christmas morning came that year and I just

knew that bike would be waiting for me. After all, I'd written Santa five times.

And yet, none of the gifts were Princess-Sparkle-Unicorncycle sized. They were package-of-ten-socks sized. They were Barbie-doll sized. They were pajamas-from-grandma sized.

My mom got a new vacuum.

My dad got a birdhouse.

My brothers got Nerf guns.

All was lost.

The last gift under the tree was a small brown envelope with my name scribbled on it. It couldn't hold a bike, what did I care?

"Says go to the garage," my dad said with a grin.

I sprinted through the sea of boxes and shredded paper, heart pounding with renewed hope—*this was it!* Only when I got to the garage, it wasn't. Not really. Yes, there was a bike. But there was no unicorn horn or rainbow tail. No tassels. It was purple, had pegs, and hanging on one handle was a pink helmet. I deflated a little but put on a brave face as I snapped the helmet on my head.

Then, a Christmas miracle: My plastered-on smile turned to a real one the second I pedaled out the driveway and down the street to my best friend's house (who spent the morning riding on the pegs I didn't know I needed). I was a kid on a bike—though not the one I dreamed of—and life was perfect.

It wasn't until years later that I found out in the weeks before that Christmas, the Princess Sparkle Unicorncycle had been recalled for safety issues. It turns out, having a tail hanging into the spokes of a spinning tire causes a little bit of an issue.

I haven't thought of that bike in years, but this season has dug up all kinds of weird memories, this bike included. I had nothing I wanted and yet I was happy—really, truly happy. Much like this year.

My mission of the season was to uncover what magic—if any—remains if we distance ourselves from the things we've always done to celebrate Christmas. If I'm honest, I was hellbent on proving nothing would be left without doing the things we've always done.

I was convinced without the people we always spend time with and the traditions we always practice, there was absolutely no point of the season. In my narrow mind, it was black and white.

Because you, my wonderful readers, are far smarter than I am, I'm assuming most of you already knew I was wrong. Most of you probably read along and laughed at my ignorance. If you are one of the few like me who were a bit stubborn to budge on this stance, I'll say it clearly: I got it all wrong.

Not only does so much remain, there's so much room for growth. For reflection. For more.

I still believe Christmas is about traditions, but it's the intention that matters more. Why are we showing up in our sweaters with pans of cookies? Is it because we care or because we care what other people think? Because we love it or we love the idea of it? Because it's what we want to do or what we've always done?

The season, you see, is far from black and

white. It's an iridescent blend of reds, greens, and every other color that does or doesn't shine from a strand of lights. It changes based on the light, on where we stand, on what we need.

No two seasons are the same, just like no two Christmases will be. Whether the season greets us holding all our shattered pieces as we weep in a bowling alley or filled with so much joy we can barely contain it while we clap along Main Street looking for Santa, Christmas will bring with it what we need as long as we are willing to see it.

Maybe it's a holiday club where you get to choose the way you celebrate.

Maybe it's watching *Die Hard* at a drive-in.

Or, just maybe, it's meeting someone who teaches you to lean into all the possibilities of traditions not yet formed.

And while this season I wasn't longing for material gifts, I'm wondering if my expectations were a bit like they were for that bike. I was so focused on what a perfect Christmas was supposed to look like for *me*—the traditions, the order of things, the very specific people doing these very specific things—that I had forgotten that it might not be what everyone else wanted it to look like. Maybe not even what I wanted it to look like when I really thought about it.

All these years later, I know I ended up with the right bike. The gift I got instead of the one I wanted was exactly what I needed. It was perfect, really. Just like this Christmas.

I barged my way into The Holiday Club looking for one thing but finding another, forever changing how I will celebrate the holidays for the rest of my life.

Merry Christmas, dear readers. I hope this season gives you everything you didn't know you needed.

Acknowledgments

Not to be cliché, but this story was such a joy to write. As in most of my books, there's a little bit of me in here. The mom that wants to do everything at the holidays because FOMO is real and everyone else is doing it too? I've been that crazy person more than once. Like always when I notice my most cringy parts coming to the surface in my writing, I got a good laugh. I hope you did too.

Thank you, as always, to my first readers for helping me get this story to where it is now. Thanks for everything, especially your time, but mostly the laughs.

Big love to my editors, Victoria Straw, Kaitlin Slowik, and Sadie Tabolt for getting this story reader ready, and to my cover artist, Elise Stamm, for always bringing my blurry ideas to life. Thank you isn't big enough.

And, of course, my family—Kevin, Oak, and Vale—for supporting me both in every writing project I think up and every wild idea I have around the holidays. My pink Christmas tree and I will be forever in your debt.

Lastly, to my haggish readers. Y'all are some of the best gifts I've ever gotten.

Also, Marv's code could be cracked, but you might need to look at a flip phone to do it. Cheers!

About Ashley

Ashley Manley is a current writer and former just about everything else. When she isn't stringing words together on her computer, you can find her chasing her kids, reheating her coffee, or dreaming of her next grand adventure under tall trees. While she's lived a little bit of everywhere, North Carolina will always feel like home. To connect with Ashley, visit ashleymanleywrites.com or find her on Instagram @ashleymanleywrites.

Other books by Ashley
Every Beautiful Mile
When Wildflowers Bloom

Life on the Ledge Duet
Forever and Back (June's book)
Now to Forever (Scotty's book)

Made in United States
Troutdale, OR
11/21/2025